The MANY Reflections of Miss JANE DEMING

The MANY
Reflections
of Miss
JANE
DEMING

J. ANDERSON COATS

 ATHENEUM BOOKS FOR YOUNG READERS
NEW YORK LONDON TORONTO SYDNEY NEW DELHI

ATHENEUM BOOKS FOR YOUNG READERS

An imprint of Simon & Schuster Children's Publishing Division

1230 Avenue of the Americas, New York, New York 10020

ATHENEUM BOOKS FOR YOUNG READERS is a registered trademark of Simon & Schuster, Inc.

Atheneum logo is a trademark of Simon & Schuster, Inc.

For information about special discounts for bulk purchases, please contact Simon & Schuster Special Sales at 1-866-506-1949 or business@simonandschuster.com.

The Simon & Schuster Speakers Bureau can bring authors to your live event. For more information or to book an event, contact the Simon & Schuster Speakers Bureau at 1-866-248-3049 or visit our website at www.simonspeakers.com.

Book design by Debra Sfetsios-Conover and Irene Metaxatos

The text for this book was set in Goudy Oldstyle Std.

Manufactured in the United States of America

0117 FFG

First Edition

10 9 8 7 6 5 4 3 2 1

Library of Congress Cataloging-in-Publication Data

Names: Coats, J. Anderson (Jillian Anderson), author.

Title: The many reflections of Miss Jane Deming / J. Anderson Coats.

Description: First Edition. | New York : Atheneum Books for Young Readers, [2017] | Summary: "Jane is excited to be part of Mr. Mercer's expedition to bring orphans and Civil War widows to Washington Territory, but life out west isn't at all what she expected"—Provided by publisher.

Identifiers: LCCN 2016007664

ISBN 978-1-4814-6496-3

ISBN 978-1-4814-6498-7 (eBook)

Subjects: | CYAC: Frontier and pioneer life—Washington (State)—Fiction. | Washington Territory—History—19th century—Fiction. | Orphans—Fiction. | BISAC: JUVENILE FICTION / Historical / United States / Civil War Period (1850-1877). | JUVENILE FICTION / Girls & Women. | JUVENILE FICTION / Family / Alternative Family.

Classification: LCC PZ7.1.C62 Man 2017 | DDC [Fic]—dc23 LC record available at https://lccn.loc.gov/2016007664

To my mom and dad

1

MRS. D SAID TO LEAVE THE PACKING TO HER, BUT when she wasn't looking, I pulled out a half-size carpetbag I made from a flour sack and put in the things I don't trust her with.

My lucky hopscotch stone.

Three hairpins I found in the big girls' yard behind the schoolhouse from back when I went to school.

The little book Miss Bradley made for me from folded sheets of cheap blank ragpaper that she stitched up the spine with packing cord.

We've been staying at Lovejoy's Hotel in New York City for two days before I get careless and go through my secret carpetbag when Mrs. D is only halfway out the door.

In three steps she's standing over me, holding out her hand. "I must have that paper, Jane."

"Why?" I ask, and it's a perfectly reasonable question, but her brows twitch and her mouth goes tight and straight.

Usually when Mrs. D makes that face, it's followed by her telling me how easy it would be for her to entrust my growing-up years to a Mother who keeps one of the mill-run boardinghouses back in Lowell. Those mills are desperate for girls to stand behind the looms now that the war is over.

Instead, she sighs like I'm simple. "In case I need to write to Mr. Mercer about the voyage. Now, do as you're told."

Mrs. D hasn't exactly *told* me to do anything, and it's not like she can write real good anyway.

"The pages are all filled up," I reply, and I show her the ones at the front that are covered with copy exercises and sums.

She narrows her eyes but lets me keep it.

There are exactly seven blank pages at the end, but there's no reason Mrs. D has to know that. It won't be long before this little book will be useful once more.

We're a week at Lovejoy's before another member of Mr. Mercer's expedition arrives. She's called Miss Gower, and she barely gets through her nice-to-meet-yous before she tells us she already wrote to Washington's territorial governor to ask that she be officially recognized as the Old Maid of the Territory.

There's a pained silence. Being an old maid is akin to having a dire sickness or expecting a baby—something you don't mention in polite company. Mrs. D looks faintly disgusted, like she's about to change a very full diaper, but I blurt, "What did he say?"

"Hsst!" Mrs. D gives me a Look. "Children should be seen and—"

"He agreed, of course." There's more than a hint of pride in Miss Gower's voice and half a chortle. "It's best to call things as they are, and an old maid is definitely what I am and will remain, come what may. What should I call you?"

"Who? Me?"

Miss Gower nods. She's not even looking at Mrs. D.

"J-Jane." I stand a little straighter, like I'm back at school giving a recitation. "Ma'am."

"My stepdaughter," Mrs. D adds with a sigh, "who really ought to know better than to speak to her elders in such a way."

Whenever Mrs. D says things like this, I try not to giggle or roll my eyes. She's only two and twenty, and she doesn't look old enough to say things like *Children should be seen and not heard.*

She means them, though.

"This little charmer is my son, Jeremiah. We call him Jer." Mrs. D turns Jer toward Miss Gower, since this is usually the part where grown-ups coo and make a sappy face to get him to smile.

Miss Gower's brows twitch. "I so dislike the prefix *step.* It implies partitions in a family that holy wedlock should render obsolete."

Papa said almost the same thing on their wedding day. *We're all Demings now. Steps are for walking down.*

"Hmm. Well." Mrs. D smiles all tight-lipped and pointy. "Do pardon us. The baby needs his rest. Jane?"

"Yes, ma'am." As I close the door, Miss Gower is shaking her head like she just saw something impossible or ridiculous or both.

I like to think Papa would do something akin to that if he were still alive. That he'd notice Mrs. D sighing over my sawdusty bread and dirty fingernails and ask her to help me mix better or scrub harder instead of complain. He'd have surely given back all the dolls and skipping ropes and other *childish things* she made me hand over the day she had Jer. I like to think he'd be taking my side.

♔ ♔ ♔

Mr. Mercer comes by the hotel again today to assure us we'll be under way anytime now, bound for Washington Territory, where there are limitless opportunities for individuals of excellent character and the climate is positively Mediterranean. A number of us in his expedition are staying at Lovejoy's, waiting for him to complete the arrangements.

The steamship was supposed to sail back in September. January's half over, and we've heard *anytime now* since Christmas. No one wants to say what at least some of us are thinking: Perhaps Mr. Mercer is a confidence man who has pocketed our passage money and plans to run off with it.

If that were true, though, he'd surely be long gone by now. No, he's probably trying to find just the right ship. It will need to be grand if it's to fit the seven hundred unmarried girls and war widows Mr. Mercer plans to bring out west to teach in the schools of Washington Territory or to turn their hands to other useful employment.

Or, if you are Mrs. D, marry one of the many prosperous gentlemen bachelors pining for quality female society.

She's pinned all her hopes on it. Mrs. D hated working in the Lowell mills. She hated leaving her kitchen and hearth and standing for fourteen hours a day before a loom, sneezing from all the dust and lint and not being able to sleep at night because of the ringing in her ears. She wants to be a wife again, to have someone else go out to work while she keeps house. If she has to go all the way to Washington Territory to do it, by golly, that's what she'll do.

After Mrs. D paid our passage, Mr. Mercer gave her a copy of a pamphlet he wrote about the advantages and charms of Washington Territory. She glanced at it once, rolled her eyes, then left it on her chair in the dining room. I snatched it up and hid it in my secret carpetbag, and when she's not around, I read it.

I've read every word hundreds of times. Even the big words I must puzzle over. Even the boring chapters on Lumber and Trade.

My favorite part is the last chapter, Reflections Upon the Foregoing, where Mr. Mercer writes about the sort of person who would want to go to Washington Territory. An unspoiled and majestic place, he says, a place ideally suited to men of broad mind and sturdy constitution who seek to make a home through industry and wit.

The same must be true for girls of broad mind and sturdy constitution. Otherwise Mr. Mercer would never think to bring us out there. My constitution is sturdy enough. After Jer was born, I got strong hauling buckets of water and scrubbing diaper after diaper on a secondhand washboard.

The problem is my mind. It might not be suitably broad.

When Jer was just weeks old, I had to stay home from school to look after him while Mrs. D went out to work. I never much cared for school till I had something to compare it to. Suddenly all the braid-pulling boys and backside-bruising seats and longhand division and terrifying recitations in front of a frowning Miss Bradley weren't so bad after all. Not when you put it against the endless trudge of keeping house, where there's always one more thing to clean. Not when strangers on the street call you *poor dear* and cluck and sigh over all the fatherless children.

Beatrice was the first of my friends who stopped coming around. Jer cried the whole visit, and I couldn't even offer tea because the fire kept going out. Not that there was anything to talk about. I didn't know the new girl at school, and Beatrice didn't care how hard it was to dry diapers when the weather was damp.

Elizabeth and Violet didn't make it past the threshold.

It could have been different. It *should* have been different. Papa and Mrs. D were married when the war was going to be over by Christmas. Of 1861.

In Washington Territory they probably barely even knew there *was* a war. Just stepping off the boat in a place like that will give all of us what we want. Mrs. D will have her hearth. Jer will have his mama. Since she's set on remarrying, better it be to a man who made his way west before any shots were fired on Fort Anywhere. A man with all his limbs, who doesn't cringe when there's a sudden loud noise. He'll step right out of the chapter on Trade, maybe, or Civil Government, tall and handsome and happy to give Mrs. D whatever she wants, so she'll smile at me and mean it, then tell me to run along and play and be home in time for supper.

I will have ordinary chores and lots of friends. I will have a dress that fits. I'll spend my days in a schoolhouse instead of being someone's *little mother*, as the mill girls would say. I will have limitless opportunities because of my sturdy constitution and a mind I hope to broaden. No one will ever call me *poor dear*.

No one will ever have cause to.

It's been sleeting all morning, so Jer and I can't play outside. Jer just turned two and already he's trying to talk. Ever since we got to New York, the only thing he wants to talk about is carriages.

"Daney! Tarij. Tarij Daney *yes!*" Jer bounces on the bed in our room and points out the window at the sliver of street crowded with people and horses and wagons.

"You might *think* you want to sit out front and watch

carriages," I tell him, "but it's too cold, so what you *really* want is to hear me reread Reflections Upon the Foregoing."

"Tarij," he repeats stubbornly, so I shrug and leave him at the window and read aloud anyway.

My brother doesn't need to hear Mr. Mercer's reflections the way I do. Saying the words out loud makes Washington Territory feel like a secret that's been kept just for me, and it's going to change everything.

CHILDREN AREN'T SUPPOSED TO BE IN THE PARLOR
of Lovejoy's, but if Jer and I play quietly in the corner,
Mr. Hughes can pretend he doesn't notice us. So we're
there, building with some blocks that once belonged to
Mr. Hughes's son, when the front door bangs open and a
gust of freezing air blows a cabman into the foyer.

"I've come to collect the Mercer party," he says.
"*Continental*'s ready for 'em."

Mr. Hughes sighs and nods, then sends the bellboy
upstairs with the news. Although he tries to hide it, Mr.
Hughes considers us all fools for believing in Mr. Mercer's
expedition. He thinks we'll come to a bad end, and he's
too polite to say it, but he has Opinions on the sort of
girl or woman who would volunteer to travel all the way

around Cape Horn to a town on the edge of the world and take up residence there.

I have Opinions on the sort of person who considers someone else's decision foolish just because he wouldn't make the same one.

It's water under the bridge now. I leap up and sing, "The ship is here!"

"Ship! Ship!" Jer rushes for the door like the ship is waiting in the gutter. I chase him down, and we put away the blocks. Mostly, I put them away while Jer squeals *ship* and dances like a monkey.

Things feel different already. My hands are starting to turn skin-colored again, and my nails are growing past my fingertips for the first time in ages. I haven't washed a dish or a diaper in weeks. Sending out the laundry isn't cheap, but there's nowhere to wash anything in a hotel. Even though Mrs. D complains like it hurts her bodily, every week she's been misering out coins from the bottom of her purse to the hollow redheaded girl who picks up our dirty laundry and brings it back clean and pressed.

The girl is my age. Her feet are bare and raw, and her forearms are covered with flatiron burns both fresh and healed-over. She won't look at me or Mrs. D or even Jer. When we first moved in, I thought maybe she'd like to play hopscotch sometime. I told her my name and made a joke to coax her to look up. She did—for half a moment, sidelong—but her eyes were empty, like a cart horse or a dairy goat.

That was me once. That's how everyone in Lowell saw me. That's why I wasn't even Jane Deming anymore, only *poor dear*.

Never again. Not in Washington Territory.

Outside the hotel, a wagon and a carriage are holding up traffic. Jer is puppy-wiggle happy just being close to the muddy wheels and snorting, stamping horses. The cabman's boy packs the wagon with our trunks and carpetbags while the cabman holds open the carriage door and gestures for us to get in.

Jer's eyes go round under his little cap. "We go tarij? Daney, *tarij?*"

I grin and squeeze his hand. "We are indeed going in the carriage."

Miss Gower steps toward the mounting block the cabman has put in front of the door.

"Ma'am?" I tug her sleeve. "Would you mind if we sat by the window? My brother would dearly love to see the city go past."

"Your brother?" Miss Gower peers at me over her spectacles as if she's waiting for me to add something.

"Me too, if I'm honest."

Miss Gower steps away from the open door, and I resist the urge to hug her. She doesn't exactly look like the sort of person you hug without forewarning. Instead, I thank her and hop onto the mounting block and into the carriage. The cabman swings a squealing, delighted Jer up and onto my lap.

Before long, we arrive at the pier. The wharves are busy with crates and ropes and dockworkers, and beyond there's a sweep of green-gray water cluttered with hundreds of boats and ships. Everything smells salty and damp.

The cabman directs us toward a group gathered near a disorderly pile of trunks. There are several women on their own, but mostly it's men and families with children and couples, too. Perhaps they're waiting to send off their daughters or mothers or sisters to Washington Territory.

The cabman's boy points out the *Continental*, waiting at anchor in the river. She's made of dark wood and has two masts, front and back. In the middle is the smokestack, where steam from the engine must come out. She has the perfect name. A promise, almost: *Look how much space there is between Lowell and Washington Territory.*

Soon, sailors lower a handful of rowboats from the side of the *Continental* and glide toward the pier. I expected Mr. Mercer to oversee our boarding, but instead an officer named Mr. Vane climbs out of the first boat and gives us instructions.

While we wait our turn for a rowboat, I ask Mr. Vane, "Is the ship setting sail today? Or setting . . . steam?"

"We are, my dear. With the afternoon tide."

"How can we? Won't it take a long time to get seven hundred girls and women on the ship?"

Mr. Vane laughs. "There'll be a hundred people boarding at the very most. Not all of them girls, either. Mr. Mercer's ambitions have long since outstripped his abilities—and his funds."

There should be a chapter in Mr. Mercer's pamphlet about the sort of easterner who feels the need to run down paradise just because he or she won't get to experience it. Without this expedition I'd be stuck in Lowell and up to my elbows in diaper-stink washwater.

Not soon enough, a rowboat bumps back to the pier, and it's our turn to board. Mrs. D gives Mr. Vane a flirty smile and holds his hand a moment longer than she needs to as he helps her into the boat. I make a gag-face to Jer behind her turned back, even though he's too little to appreciate how funny it is.

More than one person—usually a preacher—has told me I should feel sorry for Mrs. D. They say she didn't ask to be a widow at twenty. She didn't ask to be left with a farm she couldn't run and a baby that looks just like his papa. She didn't ask to be forced to sell everything and grovel for a finger-crimping, soul-breaking job in a grimy mill town that has fifty women for every man, and those men ruined and scarred both outside and in.

I always *yes sir* or *yes ma'am* this not-helpful person, but I didn't ask to lose my mother when I was so little I barely remember her. I didn't ask for my father to die unremarkably in the mud during the Siege of Vicksburg or for a stepmother who sat steely-eyed when we got the news and said there'd be no crying under her roof. I didn't ask for well-meaning people to be sorry I'm fatherless, as if that's the only trouble I have, or for all this to be so common that those same people could only shake their heads sadly and murmur that phrase I've come to hate.

Poor dear.

The rowboat stops alongside the *Continental*, and we climb a rope ladder to get on board. Mr. Vane goes up one-handed, holding Jer firmly against his shoulder. Even though the ship isn't steaming yet, it sways and rolls. Mr. Vane slides Jer into my arms. I put him down so he can get used to the motion, and hold his hand tight.

The deck is crowded with passengers and sailors and officers and deckhands and baggage and hundreds of hatboxes. Mr. Vane is right. It's not just girls boarding.

Widows, children, couples, bachelors, families—all the people waiting with us on the pier are making their way aboard.

Not quite the magnificent exodus of female society Mr. Mercer always spoke of. Still, it takes a certain kind of person to move all the way out west, so perhaps it's a good thing there won't be seven hundred. Mr. Mercer is wise to be choosy in who he allows to join this expedition.

"Mr. Mercer said we would all be in staterooms." Mrs. D shines her pretty-headtilt smile at Mr. Vane. "Can you tell us which one is ours?"

"Staterooms are all on the main deck." He swings a leg over the side and starts climbing down the rope ladder toward the rowboat. "Cross the promenade deck—that way—and go down the portside ladder."

"Wait!" Mrs. D flails her hands. "What—where—where is Mr. Mercer?"

"No notion, ma'am." Mr. Vane's head disappears.

Mrs. D mutters a bad word.

"Just lodge yourself in the stateroom of your choosing." Miss Gower appears at my elbow, a porter nearby with her trunk on his beefy shoulder. "If that layabout Asa Mercer can't be bothered to show his face and direct the passengers, we will do for ourselves, and he can whistle for his supper if he has no liking for it."

"Yes, ma'am," I say, even though I wish she wouldn't call him bad names when he's probably busy on shore working out the last of the arrangements.

We get to the place near the smokestack where Mr. Vane pointed, but there's no ladder. There is a set of stairs, though, so we head down and find ourselves in a long corridor that's dim and narrow. Smaller corridors lead away to the staterooms every few paces. The first door we come to that's not occupied or locked is 143.

"Finally!" Mrs. D mutters, and she throws open the door.

The ceiling is low, and most of the room is taken up by two bunk beds against one wall. The floor has been hastily and halfheartedly scrubbed so it's clean everywhere but the edges. Everything smells like damp wood and a wool dress at the end of laundry day.

"Ugh!" Mrs. D groans. "How dare they call this a stateroom? Our room at Lovejoy's was bigger. Nicer, too! Wait here, children. There's got to be a better one."

Mrs. D sways up the corridor, peeking in doorways and rattling handles. After a dozen tries she stumbles back into room 143, looking like her new-baked cake just fell on the floor.

"This'll do," she mutters. "They're all the same."

"May I have the top bunk?" I ask, because it reminds

me of the tree house in *The Swiss Family Robinson*, which my grandmother used to read out loud when she'd visit.

"You may, but Jer can't be up there."

"No up," Jer agrees, climbing onto the bottom bunk and sticking his feet through the slats.

There's a knock at the door. A deckhand is waiting in the corridor with our trunk and Mrs. D's carpetbags. While she's fussing over where to put them, I climb the ladder to my bunk and promptly bang my head because the ceiling is so low. So I hunker down and pull Mr. Mercer's pamphlet out of my own carpetbag. I open it to Reflections Upon the Foregoing and make an improvement: *men AND GIRLS of broad mind and sturdy constitution.*

"Mama? We go boat? Mama? *Mama?*"

"What a splendid idea, honeydarling. Jane will take you to look around the boat."

I peer over the side. Mrs. D is busy sorting through her stockings and petticoats in the trunk, ignoring Jer and his excited tugs to her skirts. She doesn't even realize what he's asking, so I climb down and reach for his hand.

"We already had our turn," I tell Jer as we walk up the little hall to where it meets the main corridor in the shape of a T. "We can watch other people getting on board."

Down the main corridor are more staterooms and two necessaries. One is for Ladies, the other for Gentlemen.

Jer is neither, but I take him into Ladies with me. There are bathtubs and washbasins and chamber pots. Near the corner there's a pump for water and a grate in the floor.

Even Lovejoy's didn't have an indoor necessary. This voyage just keeps getting better!

If there really are a hundred people set to board, chances are good there'll be girls my age. Girls who have never seen my hands red and cracked. Girls who have never watched through a schoolhouse window as I trudge to the public pump. Girls going the same place as me, on the same ship, so we'll always have something to talk about even once we've landed in Seattle.

Jer and I go back up to the promenade deck and dodge passengers and sailors while we wait for the ship to depart. We watch the deckhands hauling lines—one of them hears me saying *ropes* and explains that at sea every rope is a line—and try to spot the dolphins the second mate swears will follow the steamer once we're outbound.

The mate hasn't known Jer quite two minutes when he gives him a carved toy horse. Jer is the image of his small son back in Glasgow, the mate explains, and the ship could do with a few more boys just like Jer to make home feel that much closer.

"Hoss! Hoss!" Jer hugs it and does a stumbly little dance.

"Do you have a daughter, too?" I ask hopefully, but the mate thinks I'm joking and gives me a friendly wink before swaying off toward the foremast.

Jer and I are counting gulls and working on our sea legs when there's a low, deep *chunkrumble* beneath our feet.

"What dat?" Jer crouches and pats the deck.

"We're leaving," I whisper.

The pier looks like toothpicks already, New York behind it chockablock with tall buildings, and Lowell somewhere beyond that with its relentless, clattering mills that almost swallowed us up.

I have never been happier to turn my back on anything.

In just four short months we'll be in Washington Territory. A place where things are carved out brand-new from an unspoiled land beneath starry-decked heavens, with no hint of anything that came before.

I have that part of the pamphlet memorized. Mostly because it can't happen soon enough.

3

AFTER ALL OUR WANDERING WE END UP BACK in the ladies' necessary, because Jer swears up, down, and sideways he has to make water. He's only been in britches since we arrived in New York, and I pay him mind when he says he has to go because it means less washing. Now that he's here, though, he just wants to climb in the wash-tubs and play with the pump.

It does no good to rush him, so I point him at a chamber pot and hum a song about ol' Cape Horn I heard the deckhands singing. Finally Jer starts peeing, only he misses the pot completely and it trickles down the wall toward the grate in the floor.

"Good boy," I mutter, but I wish he'd hurry, because I've never been in an indoor necessary, so I don't know if other ladies will take kindly to him using the Ladies'.

There's a giggle and a clatter out in the corridor, then two girls burst in, throw the door closed, and lean against it.

I wanted to meet other girls. Just not in the necessary while my brother is pulling up his britches.

They're older than me, but no older than the big girls back at school. The girl in the blue dress shushes her giggling companion and puts her ear to the door.

"He's in the corridor." She grins wickedly. "Is he going to wait out there so he can catch us in the act?"

The other girl squints like she's listening. "No, he's going away."

That's when they start laughing like Violet and I did the day Elizabeth convinced Miss Bradley her pet skunk got loose beneath the schoolhouse, so we got extra recess while the big boys crawled under the building trying to find it.

Back when we were all still laughing together.

"We should play here." The blue-dress girl has shiny chestnut hair like Beatrice's and a no-better-than-she-should-be grin.

"Ugh, we can't play faro in the necessary!"

"You could try the music room," I say, and both of them turn as if they just realized I'm here.

"We have a music room?" The blue-dress girl has a tilt in her words that isn't New York's or even Boston's. It's not pretty or foreign like some of the mill girls', but she's clearly from a place that's as far from here as I'd like to be.

"Peeeee-ano," Jer speaks up, and when the blue-dress girl smiles and winks at him just like she might anyone, I risk a step toward them.

"The ship was supposed to hold seven hundred girls," I reply. "There's probably one of *every* room."

The blue-dress girl opens the necessary door. "I'm Nell. That's Flora. Come, show us the music room."

I hoist Jer onto my hip and head up the corridor. "Who are we running from?"

"Mr. Mercer, of course." Nell is wearing a hat Mrs. D would give her right arm for. "Old Pap thinks it's improper for girls to play cards."

They shouldn't talk about Mr. Mercer that way. If it weren't for him, none of us would be going to Washington Territory.

Nell grins and holds a door open for me. Flora gestures me through it. Both of them are right behind me. Like Elizabeth once upon a time. Like Beatrice and Violet. So I keep quiet and lead on.

The music room isn't much of a music room. It's where the deckhands were able to fit the piano one of the passengers brought with her. There are some benches and a few padded stools, but not much else save portholes that let in circles of daylight.

Nell produces a deck of cards and cocks them playfully at Flora. "You ready to lose at baccarat?"

"Hey, we were playing faro!" Flora protests. "I'm terrible at—"

"What's the meaning of this?" Mr. Mercer charges through the doorway and rips the cards out of Nell's hands. "I thought I made myself clear in this regard, Miss Stewart! There will be no impropriety from any of my charges. Your brother will be hearing from me. So will your mother, Miss Pearson."

Flora rolls her eyes, but Nell cringes and pulls in a deep shuddery breath.

Like I used to when Mrs. D got angry and swore I'd be better off a mill girl in the care of the boardinghouse Mothers, before I knew she was only talk.

I step forward. "They're mine. The cards. Not Nell's."

Mr. Mercer turns his disdain on me. "Yours? Miss . . ."

I nod, then duck my chin and curtsy. I can't have him angry at me. If I'm on this ship, it means he thinks I'm worthy of Washington Territory. We're well clear of the harbor, but maybe he could still find a way to send me back to New York.

Send all three of us back. Me and Jer and Mrs. D. There we'd be on the pier without a penny to our names while the ship steamed away without us.

"Why you all di'ty?" Jer points at Mr. Mercer, and sure enough, his frock coat is heavily smudged and his red hair streaked with black as if he just loaded ten coal stoves.

Flora slaps a hand over her grin. Nell's still studying her tight-clenched hands.

Mr. Mercer ignores Jer and shakes his head at me, slow and disgusted. "To think of the lengths I went to ensure that only the most respectable of feminine society would be introduced to Washington Territory."

I flinch, but Nell closes her eyes and swallows hard. She's clearly worried about something other than how respectable Mr. Mercer considers her.

When Mrs. D gets this way, there's only one response. I lick my lips and say, "Beg pardon, sir. I didn't mean any harm."

"There are pressing matters to which I must attend, but don't think for a moment there won't be consequences." Mr. Mercer pockets the cards, turns on his heel, and stomps down the corridor.

The moment he's gone, Nell throws her arms around me like we're long-lost sisters. Her hug gets Jer, too, and he squeals and swims in her skirts. "Thank you," Nell whispers into my hair, fierce and breathy. "You don't know how you just saved me."

When she pulls away, Flora takes my forearm with one hand and Nell's with the other. "Don't you worry, Nell. We'll get your cards back. Even if we have to sneak into Mr. Mercer's room."

I'm not sure I like the sound of that.

But I do like the sound of *we*.

Flora and Nell plan to meet on the hurricane deck at the front of the ship to work out how to get Nell's cards back. They don't exactly say that Jer's not invited, but at two different times both mention how noisy he is, so I bring Jer back to the stateroom with a plan of my own.

I feel a strong case of seasickness coming on. Mrs. D will have to take Jer while I recover.

The stateroom is empty. Mrs. D is not the sort of person who'd be curious about the ship or the view from the rail, so she must have gone to the ladies' cabin. It's a little parlor next to the dining room where there are sewing machines and divans and settles under army-looking tarps and blankets.

Sure enough, I find Mrs. D there surrounded by half a dozen married ladies and widows all chatting politely about things like dress patterns and the woeful condition of their staterooms.

I put Jer down and he toddles over to Mrs. D, squealing, "Mama! Mama!"

Mrs. D kisses him on the head, then turns to the woman mending next to her and asks, "Aren't you *terribly* excited for the voyage? I have it from Mr. Mercer himself that the bachelors of Washington Territory are up-and-coming gentlemen flocking to a region rich with opportunity. There should be plenty of *very* suitable men to go around!"

"Mama, up." Jer is trying to climb her leg like a bug on a wall. "Up."

"He's saying they're going to meet us at the pier and— Jer! Oh, you've torn out a whole row!" Mrs. D untangles him from her yarn, then calls, "Jane, where are you going? Didn't I ask you to take Jer?"

I slump in the doorway. "Ma'am? I'm seasick. Bad seasick. I should really be lying down." For about a minute. Then I'm off to the hurricane deck before you can say *Jack Robinson.*

"You're free to lie down, but you'll need to take Jer with you." Mrs. D nudges him toward me. "Honeydarling, go with Jane."

"It might be rather . . ." If I describe the seasick part

too well, she'll take me to task for being *vulgar*. If I don't do it well enough, she won't give in. ". . . messy. Ma'am."

"You can't really think he can be in here." Mrs. D sighs. "In a room full of sharp knitting needles and stray pins? Or expensive sewing machines? Honestly, Jane, use some sense."

Jer tromps toward me with his little cart horse steps.

"Please? It's just that I'm—"

"Yes. Seasick. I heard. Get a chamber pot from the necessary if you need one." Mrs. D waves me away swish-swish before turning back to her neighbor and continuing, "Mr. Mercer says there's a lot of money to be made in the territory, and the gentlemen there have everything they need but quality female society . . ."

Jer winds his arms around my knees and grins up at me.

I'm not out of plans yet. I walk Jer up and down the promenade deck till he's worn out. By the time I've made up the beds in the stateroom with the bedrolls and blankets we brought, then tucked Jer and Hoss into the bottom bunk for a nap, Nell and Flora are nowhere to be found. They're not on the hurricane deck or in the music room or the dining room or even the necessary.

Of course they're not.

They must think I didn't want to help. Maybe they

think I'm too nose-in-the-air virtuous to sneak into a gentleman's room and steal something, even something taken unfairly.

"Jane?" Flora's coming up the deck. Without Nell, she seems younger somehow, like Jer when he's lost a toy. "Good, you're all right. Thank heavens."

"Where's Nell?"

Flora studies her feet. "She's . . . resting."

The way she says it makes me think she's lying, but I haven't been acquainted with either of them long enough to argue, so I say, "Did your mother get angry? About the cards?"

"Nahhh." Flora shrugs. "My mother's too intent on getting to Washington Territory and seeing my father and my sister. I could run off with the third engineer and she'd barely notice."

"Your family's already in the territory? Did they go because of the war?"

Papa should have packed himself and me and Mrs. D onto a steamship in 1861 the moment the rebel states started seceding. There'd have been no Vicksburg to tip my family toward ruin. No looms to finish the job.

Flora shakes her head. "My father and sisters went a few years ago with the first boatload of girls brought by Mr. Mercer."

"That—really happened?" I gape. "My stepmother thought he made that story up so we'd trust him and his motives."

Flora laughs. "The newspapers did rake poor Mr. Mercer over the coals, didn't they? No, there were eleven girls who went that first trip, and my father went along as part chaperone and part fellow-traveler. Now he keeps a lighthouse along with my sister Georgie. I'm to take over for him once I arrive."

"Huh." I follow Flora up the ladder onto the hurricane deck. "You can't be much older than me. Can you really be a lighthouse keeper?"

"I'm fifteen," Flora says. "My sister was that old when she started keeping the light with my father."

I try to think of a good question to keep her talking, so she doesn't ask how old I am and I don't have to admit I'm only eleven.

"Now my father wants to make a homestead claim," Flora goes on, "and to do that you have to live on and clear the land you mean to claim. It really takes two people to keep the light, so he thinks I'd be perfect."

I lean against the rail. "Did your sisters have any trouble . . . you know. Settling in? When they got there?"

"Josie got a good teaching job right away," Flora says, "but she always had a bad heart and died not long after taking it. Georgie taught for a term, but now she's keeping the light with my father. She's got a sweetheart, and I imagine they'll get married before too long."

The gray choppy water stretches out like a promise, and the engine rumbling and chuntering under my feet is taking me to a place even better than the one Mr. Mercer promises in his pamphlet. A place where two girls can run a lighthouse and teaching jobs are so unremarkable, there must be schools everywhere.

"The best thing about the voyage for both my sisters was always the other girls," Flora adds. "Even now, Georgie's letters are simply *packed* with tidbits about who's teaching where or who's engaged to which young man and where each one is setting up house. They're all still the best of friends and probably will be till they die. Honestly, by now the other girls are almost like my sisters too."

"I always wanted a sister," I say, mostly to the rushing spray and flappeting sails.

Flora frowns. "But . . . who is that you're traveling with?"

"That's my stepmother."

"Your—I thought she was your sister!"

If I had a penny for every time I heard that, I could buy back the farmhouse and pretend it was still 1860.

Flora is quiet for a moment, then she bumps me playfully with her shoulder and says, "Will you settle for a friend who's like a sister? Or maybe two? If you can keep up with the whirlwind that is Nell Stewart?"

It's not settling. Not when you get something you want, even if it's not quite the way you thought you'd get it.

We talk for ages. Flora finds the promenade deck as delightful as I do and the deckhands as interesting, but I'm also trying to avoid indoors, because Mr. Mercer is bound to have confronted Mrs. D about the cards by now. The longer I can keep away from her, the more time she'll have to stitch her angry into shirts instead of loosing it at me. By midafternoon, though, Flora wants to go write some letters, and I should check on Jer, so we agree to find Nell and all sit together at supper.

There's no dinner because the galley wants some sorting out, so by suppertime I'm hungry enough that I'm willing to hear any number of complaints about my behavior as long as I can do it over a plate of something hot.

The dining room is called the saloon. The captain, his family, and the officers sit at a long table at the front, along with Mr. Mercer. The girls cluster at another table, married couples and families and bachelors at a third, and widows and their children at the last.

Flora is sitting with her mother, and at the far end of the table Nell is perched at the right hand of a sleek young man who's perhaps Mrs. D's age. He must be Nell's brother. His black hair is perfectly oiled and he's wearing a frock coat so plush even I know it must be expensive.

Nell's shoulders are rolled forward, and she's studying the table like it's a reader. This is not the saucy, grinning girl who proposed playing cards in the necessary.

There's a purple bruise down her jaw.

I wave to Flora and she waves back. When I get near the families' table, Mrs. Pearson nods to where the widows are sitting and says, "You'll want to join your moth—stepmother at that table, dear."

"But Jane and I have so much to talk about," Flora protests.

"Mr. Mercer insists there be no impropriety on this voyage," Mrs. Pearson replies. "We'll sit where he asks us. Poor man has enough troubles without us adding something so silly and petty."

Flora grumbles, but I say, "Yes, ma'am," and I mean it. I owe Mr. Mercer too much to worsen whatever troubles he has, even if he is going to set my stepmother on me.

"Shall we meet again tomorrow?" I ask Flora.

"I'd like that. We're room 68." She smiles at me and pokes Jer's belly to make him giggle. "I hope you're up for finishing the matter from earlier today." She tips her chin the smallest bit toward Nell. They must not have gotten Nell's cards back. Either they didn't try, or they tried and were caught.

One way or another, it's not something to discuss in front of Mrs. Pearson.

"I think so," I say, and when Flora grins like a month of sunrises, I know for sure I'm up for it.

Mrs. D sees Jer and me coming toward the widows' table and holds out her arms. "Here's my honeydarling now. Isn't he just as sweet as a big slice of sugar pie with sugar on top?"

The other widows chime in on what a honeydarling Jer is, and all around the table are sappy faces and out-stretched hands.

"Sit down, Jane. You look like a scullion." Mrs. D jabs a thumb at the empty place at the end of the bench. Before I can *yes ma'am* her, she adds, "Mr. Mercer had some interesting things to say about you earlier."

She laughs, high and cruel. My whole heart goes cold.

Then I realize she's not laughing at me. She's laughing at Mr. Mercer.

"A deck of cards!" Mrs. D snorts quietly. "Imagine, a man whose reputation is in such tatters that he had to hide in the coal bin until we were well out of New York harbor, lecturing *me* on the quality of my child-rearing."

"Am . . . am I in trouble?" I croak. "Ma'am?"

"Oh heavens, Jane!" Mrs. D sighs patiently. "Eat your supper."

"Yes, ma'am," I reply, but she's already turned to her companions and leaped back into her speculations on the bachelors of Washington Territory. Most of the widows insist they're going for useful employment rather than to simply get married, but they all seem to be paying mind to Mrs. D's delighted ramblings on the bankers and lumber tycoons waiting for them.

I can breathe again.

Across the room Nell winces as she tries to open her mouth enough to slide in a spoon. Her brother sips a glass of honey-colored liquor and surveys the saloon like we're animals in a zoo.

He's clearly taken a much dimmer view of a deck of cards than Mrs. D.

Sitting with the widows sounds like it would be boring, but they're the worst kind of gossips and I learn a number of interesting things, starting with the names of every person in the room, down to the babies, and what brings them on Mr. Mercer's expedition.

There are almost three dozen young ladies on board. During the pell-mell that was boarding, they took over a block of staterooms near the rear of the ship. Then they convinced several men and a few families who'd taken nearby rooms to move to different ones, and now they have the whole section to themselves. Mr. Mercer is taking credit for it too, and using words like *propriety* instead of *courtesy*.

Even with so many girls on the ship, not a one is my age. Flora and Nell are the closest, but four years is a lot of space to properly use the word *close*. I'm tall for my age and they think I'm at least thirteen, so my hopscotch stone had best stay in my pocket.

Nell's brother is called Thad. Their parents are dead and he is her guardian. They decided to join the expedition barely an hour before we sailed. Mrs. Grinold is convinced Thad owes money he can't pay back or perhaps is wanted by the law, but the other widows refuse to believe Mr. Mercer would allow a criminal in our midst. Although such dramatic dealings would make Thad quite interesting, if he weren't so beastly to Nell.

The widows spend the most time talking about Mr. Conant, a reporter from the *New York Times* who'll be writing dispatches about our trip that will be published for the world to read. Whatever bad things easterners want to believe about Mr. Mercer's motives—and us, for going on such an expedition—will be cleared up when they read about a sturdy, broad-minded boatful of girls, families, widows, and bachelors who simply want to step off the *Continental* in Seattle and start as clean and new as the territory itself. Remade in its image. Perfect in every way, right from the beginning.

4

JER WAKES UP WHEN IT'S STILL DARK, CRAWLS over Mrs. D, and lands on the floor like a wet bag of flour. Then he bumps around the stateroom talking to Hoss. It would be sweet, if Mrs. D didn't mumble something ominous about beauty rest.

So Jer and I go up to the promenade deck, and the deckhands teach us how to tell time by the ship's bell. When it's four bells of the morning watch—six in the morning to us landsmen—Jer and I can finally tap on the door of stateroom 68 without it being an unseemly hour.

Flora is seasick. She can't even get out of bed. I didn't think to ask what room Nell is in.

Looks like it's just Jer and me playing baby games in the cold, fogbound morning.

Again.

Since Jer and I now have nothing but time, I let him climb the promenade deck stairs by himself. The *ladder*, that is, since the deckhands told me stairs on a ship are always called ladders even when they're stairs.

We linger over breakfast. We walk up and down the corridor of the main deck and I count off the stateroom numbers, because if I can't broaden my mind yet at least I can keep it from shrinkening.

We make our way aft toward the back of the ship, Hoss galloping over this chair and that ledge. Still no sign of Nell. Perhaps she's seasick too, or trying to avoid her brother and his temper.

Just beyond the mainmast there's a lifeboat on the deck against the gunwale, and it's full of kids.

"Ooooh, they're going to get in such trouble if the captain sees," I tell Jer. Even as I'm saying it, I recognize Miss Gower standing at the head of the lifeboat. She's handing a book to the boys in the middle seat.

The kids in the lifeboat aren't misbehaving. Two small girls in the front are trying and failing to recite the alphabet. There are several boys in the middle, maybe seven or eight years old, huddled over a slate. In the back are a clutch of boys my age, snickering and shoving and pretending to study a geography text.

It's a school. There's a school going on in this lifeboat.

Miss Gower spots us and nods politely. "Good morning, Jane. Would you care to join the class?"

"Sure!" I blurt. "That is . . . yes, please, ma'am."

"Excellent. We begin at eight bells by the ship's clock. That's four sets of two peals of the bell, the one that occurs after breakfast. Please be punctual tomorrow."

Miss Gower must mean eight bells of the morning watch. It's important to say what watch the bells belong to, but I don't correct her because it's just ship time and not nearly as respectable as schoolhouse learning, so of course she might not know it.

"Um . . ." Only mill girls make vulgar noises instead of saying *yes, ma'am* or *no, ma'am* like my father taught me. "Can't I start today?"

Miss Gower glances down at Jer swinging my hand like stray line. "You are clearly indisposed at the moment. By tomorrow I imagine you will have worked out arrangements with your mother regarding your younger brother."

"He'll be quiet," I say, even though I know this isn't, strictly speaking, *true*, or even something I can promise. "He's a good boy. Jer, you'll be a good boy and sit quietly, right?"

"No." Jer beams.

"Jer!" I growl. "You'd *better* be good."

Miss Gower shakes her head. "I'm sorry, Jane. Your brother is too young for formal education. Not only will you be too distracted managing his behavior to properly pursue your studies, but he'll disrupt the entire class. You are welcome to join us when you're not supervising your brother's activities. Please excuse me."

Miss Gower hitches up her skirts and steps into the front of the lifeboat. It's hard to argue when Jer's belly-down on the deck, peeling up splinters and stuffing them into my shoes.

"Hey, Jer, you want to go see your mama?" I ask, like I'm offering candy for supper.

"Mama!" Jer bounces along the promenade deck toward the ladies' cabin.

Mrs. D is sure to be missing Jer by now. Back in Lowell she'd often go whole days without seeing him awake. She wept outright when Jer took his first steps while she was flinging shuttles, and she's always saying how Jer is *so precious* because he's all she's got left of Papa.

Like I need yet another reminder I take after my mother—tall and bony, with hair that won't curl with any amount of heat or grease.

Mrs. D paces at the top of the portside ladder, hands on hips. "Where have you *been?*"

I don't dare ask about *arrangements* now. "I went to

find my friend Flora, but she's seasick and—"

"You've shirked enough for today. Mr. Mercer would have the ladies make socks to sell once we reach Seattle. It'll make us a little money and show off our many talents."

Bachelors must be woefully easy to impress. I follow Mrs. D down the ladder, but when I get to the doorway of the ladies' cabin, I ask, "Wasn't I supposed to keep Jer away from here? All the sharp things?"

"Oh, nonsense, girl." Mrs. Grinold opens her sewing basket. "Bring the little darling in. It's not as if any of us don't know how to manage small children."

Mrs. D glances at her uncertainly. Then she waves a hand at me. "Quite right, Mrs. Grinold, quite right. Jane, bring Jer in. No need to coddle him."

The cabin is stuffy and the light is struggling at best. It's all widows and a few married ladies and babies too little to run around on deck. And me.

I wait till Mrs. D has finished her favorite prediction, how a rich banker will catch sight of her on the Seattle pier and fall instantly in love with her.

"Ma'am?"

"Yes, Jane? What is it now?"

"A school started today. In the portside lifeboat. I was hoping I could go."

Mrs. D shakes out more yarn. "A school? Hmm. Every day? Not all day, surely."

"No, ma'am. Just in the mornings."

"I see. That might be all right. Who's the teacher?"

I can't tell her. I can't *not* tell her.

"I believe Adelaide Gower is presiding over the make-shift school," Mrs. Grinold says. "None of these young ladies was in any hurry to take up her vocation. Too many officers to make eyes at."

"Miss Gower. Well. Hmm." Mrs. D starts knitting again. "You can read and write and cipher just fine, Jane. I didn't even go to school, and what's good enough for me is good enough for you."

Mrs. D said something very similar to Miss Bradley when she called at our lodgings in Lowell to find out why I hadn't been coming to school. I stood behind Mrs. D with baby Jer on my arm, and Miss Bradley must have seen right away there'd be no changing Mrs. D's mind.

That was when Miss Bradley slipped me the little book with all its blank pages and whispered, "Good luck."

The other ladies are stitching or knitting most industriously. The whole room is silent. Not even Mrs. Grinold, who dismissed Mrs. D's ridiculous reasons for keeping Jer out of the ladies' cabin, will look at me.

I can't blame them for wanting no part of Mrs. D's

harsh tongue. Only, they're the ones she might listen to.

I sit down and mutter, "Yes, ma'am."

Mrs. D nods. "Good. Now, come sit here and I'll teach you a cable pattern."

It takes most of the morning to learn the pattern, but by dinnertime I've got it down.

"Wonderful!" Mrs. D says, and for once she isn't being false or snide. "You keep up that good work, child. We're going to make a fortune on that Seattle pier with these beauties." Lower, she adds, "Believe you me, we're going to need it."

After dinner I'm ready to turn the heel on the first sock. The pair will be a decent piece of work, even if they're made for a man and ridiculously large. A logging-man might buy them, or maybe a miner.

Later, lying in my top bunk and nursing stiff fingers and a sore backside, I pull out Mr. Mercer's pamphlet and reread the chapter on Trade. There are several paragraphs on things that might be made, bought, or sold, but nothing about socks.

I improve the chapter by adding a number of lines in the margin about the benefits and virtues of handmade garments and how each and every loggingman, farmer, sailor, and miner needs at least ten pairs to keep him fit for work. I finish with: *The best time to make socks is in the afternoon, once the mind has been suitably exercised and hopefully broadened.*

I should make a pair of socks for Flora. A lighthouse keeper's feet will probably get cold as well. It's something a friend who's like a sister would do.

That gives me an idea.

5

"WHY NOT?" I ASK, AND IF I'M HONEST IT'S MORE of a whine. "He's no trouble. Really!"

Flora snorts. "Five minutes ago you had to convince him to stop eating crusts he found under the tables. When he didn't like hearing that, he flung them at you."

We're in the saloon, and the scullions are clearing up the breakfast dishes. Jer is under our table, eating the crusts I dodged. The ship's bell will ring any moment now.

Nell comes up to us. She missed breakfast, and the bruise on her jaw is now a ghastly pale green, but she puts one arm around Flora's waist and the other around mine. "Are we ready to take care of that small matter, girls?"

We. I smile in spite of myself.

"Not yet, more's the pity." Flora tips her head at Jer. "Also, Jane wants to go to Miss Gower's primary school for little kids, and she wants me to watch her half brother because her stepmother's a harpy and won't do it."

Flora says *primary school* like it's something she outgrew with diapers and teething straps. I can't even enjoy learning a new thing to mutter under my breath at Mrs. D.

"Jer is my *brother*," I say curtly. "He's not half of anything."

Nell scoffs something dark about brothers being half of *something*, but then she grins. "I'll watch him. After we've gotten my cards back from you-know-who."

We both stare at her. Nell in her fancy ruffled bodice and shiny bone-buttons does not look like the sort of girl who'd willingly agree to wipe sticky fingers and play hide the thimble.

"Although I can't imagine why you'd want to go to *school* instead of playing cards," Nell singsongs. "I never took you for a schoolma'am in training."

"I promised my father I'd get a leaving certificate," I reply quietly, and it's the last thing I promised him too, when he came home for his furlough just before he got sent to Vicksburg. "That's why."

Flora ducks her head. Her father was too old to join

a regiment, her brother too young. The worst thing that happened to her because of the war was having to wear linen drawers instead of cotton.

I touch my hopscotch stone in my pocket. Then I take a deep breath and add, "It's irksome when someone decides she knows what you want just because it's what she wants. It's unkind."

Nell's smile quiets. "I'm only teasing, Jane. Forgive me. I don't mean to be unkind, especially about something one of my friends thinks is worthwhile."

Maybe if I hadn't promised Papa I'd leave school properly, I might not care either. Yet every day I'm not on a bench with a reader in my hands, that promise presses a little harder.

Nell just called me her friend.

"Now then." Nell motions both of us closer. "I have it on good authority that Mr. Mercer is staying in stateroom 4. An *officer's* berth, if you can believe such a thing. I just saw him pestering Julia Hood to walk with him on the promenade deck, so we'll have some time."

"Well, best of luck. I'll have to stay behind." I nod at Jer, who's trying to balance Hoss on a bench rung. "He couldn't possibly go with us. You both said as much."

Nell grins. "That's where you're wrong. I've been thinking it over. If we get caught, what could be a better excuse than *Ohhh, the baby ran in here and we were just getting him back?* So we need you in particular, Jane. We really can't do this without you."

When sneaking into Mr. Mercer's stateroom was just a silly thing Nell tossed out on a lark, the whole idea felt daring and exciting. Now that we're outside his door, I almost wish I were making socks right now.

"Shhhhh!" I remind Jer, and he puts his finger to his lips and goes *shhhhh* right after me.

Mr. Mercer's stateroom is at least three times bigger than ours. There's a single bed, perfectly made, and a trunk and a washstand, and *room to move around*.

Flora barely makes it over the threshold. Her feet are as cold as mine. Nell goes right to Mr. Mercer's trunk and throws it open. She starts pawing through his clothing so casually, it takes me a long moment to realize exactly what she's doing—handling shirts and waistcoats and perhaps even *undergarments* belonging to a man she hardly knows.

Nell has a sturdier constitution than I ever will.

I keep hearing footsteps in the corridor that aren't there. This is where the officers stay, but during the day they're on deck with the older girls, flirting or being gallant or whatever it is they do.

"Nell?" Flora whispers.

"Shhhhhh!" hisses Jer.

Nell holds up a pair of britches and chokes on a laugh. I giggle too, because britches are downright foolish-looking when they're big and floppy and not tiny like Jer's. Nell plunges her hands into both pockets but comes up with nothing.

"Everything's folded," she complains. "What a fuss-and-feathers dandy! Someone come fold things back up while I keep looking."

Flora shakes her head. "I'm hopeless at it."

"I can do it," I reply, which I hope is true, because I want to be *someone* for Nell. "If Flora will hold Jer."

"Down," Jer says, and I put him down right away, because if he starts squawking we're done for.

Nell shoves a pair of britches at me. "Hurry."

I fold. I pretend I'm the redheaded laundry girl back in New York, just doing a job. Flora pokes through the frock coats hanging from pegs on the wall. We're almost at the bottom of the trunk with nothing to show for it when Jer tugs on my skirt. He's holding a carpetbag very much like mine, only made of silky patterned brocade and not a faded flour sack.

"Your bag, Daney," he says. "Shhhhhh!"

"Jer, where did you get this?" I gasp. "Put it back right now!"

Nell kneels and takes the bag. "Thank you, Master Deming. You might well have saved the day."

Jer smiles his charming, rascally smile.

Sure enough, Nell's cards are stuffed next to a well-thumbed Bible and a half-written sermon on the evil vice of gambling and how it warps a girl's delicate nature.

"If Old Pap thinks faro and whist count as gambling," Nell mutters as she and I finish rearranging Mr. Mercer's clothing, "he's clearly got a lot to learn about vice."

"Can we go, please?" Flora whispers.

Nell puts Mr. Mercer's carpetbag next to his bed, and we flee down the hallway, Jer reminding us to *shhhh* every other step.

We make it back to the promenade deck before Nell looks at me and I look at her and Flora looks at both of us, and we all start laughing. Cackling, more like, and falling together in a tangly sort of hug with Jer right in the middle of it.

We got Nell's cards back. No one fainted. No one backed out. No one got caught.

All of us together.

We.

It's long past eight bells, but Nell says a promise is a promise, and she takes Jer's hand. I don't have the heart to tell her that I'm so late Miss Gower might not let me stay.

"I'll teach him his numbers by dinner," Nell says with a wink, which means she's going to take Jer to play cards with Flora, like it's the most natural thing in the world.

Miss Gower raises one eyebrow as I edge near the lifeboat.

"I'm sorry, ma'am," I tell her. "Arrangements took me a little longer than I thought."

"Hmm." Miss Gower hands me a reader. "In light of the circumstances, your tardiness is excused this time. Please be punctual in the future or there will be consequences. Now then. Open to page three and read from the top, so I might determine your current proficiency."

"Yes, ma'am!" I fumble with the reader, since the pages are blowing sharp from the wind off the starboard beam. "The . . . pig . . ."

The first page goes all right. Miss Gower has me skip to page eight, and that one's fine too. When I turn to page thirty, the words become a clutter of letters stuck together in ways I stumble and trip over.

It's been only two years since I was in school. I should remember more.

My mind is nowhere near broad enough for Washington Territory.

Miss Gower doesn't smirk or sigh. She merely says,

"Begin on page eight. This section here, about the boy cutting wood."

My eyes are stinging, but I bend over the reader. I can do this. There's still time.

Pretty soon I'm right there with the boy and his dull axe. There's even a hollow thudding somewhere behind me, as if the promenade deck were the snowy wood from page nine, but then Miss Gower says sharply, "Mrs. Deming, what—?"

Someone grabs my elbow and drags me harsh and grating over the side of the lifeboat.

"Mrs. Deming, that's hardly necessary," Miss Gower says sternly. "You could have simply asked your daughter to exit the boat."

"I hardly think so. Jane does not always do as she's told. If she did, she wouldn't be here." Mrs. D swings to face me, Jer clinging to her hand. "Jane, why did I find Jer in the company of that . . . Nell Stewart . . . person?"

Everything I can think to say will just make her more angry.

"Because that haughty minx said you had better things to do than mind him. And she had the nerve to tell me I ought to mind my own child and not impose on you so much." Mrs. D's eyes narrow. "Tell me, Jane. Do I impose on you?"

I shake my head. I stare at my feet.

"Because it sounds to me as if you were the one *imposing*," Mrs. D goes on, "when you asked a chit like her to mind Jer so you could swan about while others of us are working hard so there'll be a little money in our pockets come Seattle."

"With the *socks*?" I blurt, because the idea that Seattle men will clamor for hundreds of socks and make our fortune seems silly even for her.

"Yes, with the *socks*," Mrs. D mimics. "I don't think it's too much to ask that you work to help this family." Her voice drops to a whisper-hiss. "We get off this boat with *nothing*, Jane. The only reason we are even *aboard* this ship is Mr. Mercer's charity. Do you really think a handful of coins from the mills kept us all those weeks in Lovejoy's? Or paid for a trip halfway round the world?"

Mr. Mercer has always been so full of high-minded talk about enriching the territory with our presence that I figured he was arranging everyone's passage out of civic-mindedness. It feels blasphemous to think *money* changed hands at any point for such a noble cause.

"Mrs. Deming, you are disrupting my school," Miss Gower says. "Please take your leave."

"Gladly. Jane, let's go." Mrs. D holds Jer out at arm's length and he lands on my hip.

"Your daughter won't be remaining?"

"No. *Now*, Jane."

Miss Gower clears her throat. "It's my understanding—"

"Frankly, I could give two figs what you understand," Mrs. D cuts in. "Unless you can teach Jane to knit faster, she can learn nothing useful from you, and that's the end of it. Good day."

I should have known Nell watching Jer would never pass muster with Mrs. D. Only a fool pins all her hopes on something that sounds too good to be true.

After I put Jer to bed, I go up to the promenade deck in the hope that Flora or Nell might be there and we can amuse ourselves watching the older girls trying to ignore the stink of the whale-oil lanterns as they flirt with the officers. I'm pulling three deck chairs out of the shadows when Nell appears at the top of the starboard ladder, out of breath and glancing over her shoulder every other step.

I rush over to her. "I'm so sor—"

She cuts me off with a fierce, lingering hug. "You're not angry, are you? About your brother? I'd keep him for you. I really would. But . . ."

I sigh. "Yes. I know, *but*. Thanks anyway."

"Forget about school and come to whist instead," Nell

says. "Now that I've got my cards back, Ida May Barlow and Libbie Peebles say we can join their game. Some of the girls have taken over a whole stateroom, and they use it just for cards. There's a secret knock and everything."

"My stepmother says I have to make socks to sell in Washington Territory," I reply glumly. "All day. Every day. So I can't play. I'm sorry."

"I thought the harpy planned to have all the wealthy bachelors of Seattle eating out of her hand from the moment she stepped on the pier," Nell teases. "Maybe she's hoping to impress a textile magnate?"

"You should see her." I try to match Nell's grin. "Petting each pair of socks as she finishes them as if she's putting money in the bank."

"Or almost—oh, drat!" Nell's eyes widen, and she squeezes my arm before darting off toward the hurricane deck.

Thad comes around the corner, scanning like a bloodhound. He stomps past me in a cloud of cigar smoke. Mr. Mercer trails behind him. They're arguing about an *incident*, and they're clearly looking for Nell.

I'll lie. I'll say I haven't seen her all night. A guardian should be guarding. He should be taking Nell's side.

Neither Thad nor Mr. Mercer even glances at me.

They find Nell soon enough. The whole ship's company can hear the row. Thad, roaring that Nell is a thief and a liar and a whole lot worse. Nell, her voice wavering, shouting that she's the one who's been wronged. Mr. Mercer, telling them both to be civil. Then Thad harshly saying they can both be hanged for all he cares.

Girls and officers keep discussing the moon or music or the news from papers brought from New York, pretending not to hear. But we do. We hear every vicious, hateful word.

At the widows' table in the saloon the next morning, I'm amusing Jer by making my knife and fork dance while we wait for porridge. Flora and Nell sit elbow-to-elbow at the families' table, giggling over something and pointing at Mr. Mercer, who's three places down from the captain. Thad is reading a newspaper and sipping coffee. It's as if the hideous row last night never happened.

Miss Gower comes into the saloon, and instead of sitting where she always does, she plants herself across from Mrs. D.

"The lifeboat school is in need of an invigilator for the smallest pupils," Miss Gower tells her without so much as a *good morning*, "and it's my understanding your daughter was employed before our departure and knows a measure of hard work."

"Stepdaughter." Mrs. D sips from her dented tin army mug. "Besides, I'd hardly call keeping house *work*, and Jane has other respon—"

"The rate of pay will be a dollar a week."

I sit up straighter.

Mrs. D narrows her eyes. "A dollar a week. For in—invegetable—invid—sitting in a lifeboat?"

"Invigilate. From the Latin, meaning *to watch*." Miss Gower might be fighting a smirk. "The youngest children need extra *watching*, Mrs. Deming."

Mrs. D squinches her nose and scowls at her mug, then starts counting on her fingers. She can't cipher in her head, but I can. A dollar a week over a four-month voyage makes . . . sixteen dollars.

Sixteen whole *dollars*. We'd have to knit with pure gold yarn to make that much from socks.

"All right," Mrs. D finally says, "but only if you hand Jane's earnings to me directly. I wouldn't trust a girl this age to keep her own head on if it wasn't attached to her neck." She laughs like they're sharing a joke, but Miss Gower's face doesn't change.

"This means your son will need to stay with you while she is in my employ. I am paying for your daughter's undivided attention during this time."

"I understand." Mrs. D smiles, all teeth.

Miss Gower turns to me and asks, "Is this arrangement suitable to you?"

What would be suitable is for one of the older girls to agree to run the lifeboat school. A girl Mrs. D has no quarrel with. That girl would hand me a reader, and I'd turn right to page eight, and I'd busy myself broadening my own mind and keeping a promise I'm a little sorry I made.

But grown-ups don't often ask what I think, and if they do, they want to hear *yes, ma'am* or *no, ma'am*. They don't look me in the eye or use words like *arrangement* and *suitable*. I've also never heard anyone call minding little kids what it is—a measure of hard work.

So I say, "Yes, ma'am," and I sort of mean it.

"Then you will present yourself every morning at the lifeboat at precisely eight bells," Miss Gower replies. "You begin today, and you will be dismissed when the day's tasks are completed. If that's acceptable to your mother."

Mrs. D gives that gritty smile again. "When can I expect wages paid?"

"Every other Saturday." Miss Gower barely glances at her. "Right, Jane. I'll see you in a little while."

Breakfast ends around the seventh bell, so I have half an hour before I must report to the lifeboat. Mrs. D leads Jer away toward the ladies' cabin, him chattering and happy about spending the morning with his mama.

I head right for Nell. I must be a mess of worry, because she leans close and whispers, "I'm fine. Really. Old Pap's got no proof. The whole thing last night looked worse than it was. Thad had been drinking. He's all bark and no bite. Really."

"All right," I reply, but Thad looks plenty capable of bite, and Nell's saying *really* too much for my liking.

Flora shoulder-bumps me. "Hurrah! You can play cards now!"

"The harpy's minding her own child?" Nell asks dryly. "The ground doesn't feel nearly cold enough."

I shake my head and tell them my news.

"Huh." Flora squints. "I wouldn't think an experienced bluestocking teacher like Miss Gower would need a helper for just ten children."

Ida May Barlow leans into the saloon and holds up her reticule.

"Try to come to whist later!" Nell calls over her shoulder as Flora drags her toward the door. "Beg the harpy!" She says it like it would do a darn bit of good.

Invigilating isn't hopscotch and it's not playing cards, but at least I don't have to make socks with Mrs. D all morning.

Besides, a dollar a week is a lot of money. Miss Gower wouldn't hire an invigilator if she didn't have need of one.

6

THE SMALLER KIDS ARE BROUGHT TO THE LIFE-
boat by their mothers, while the oldest boys ramble over
just as eight bells is halfway rung. Miss Gower gives them
a Look I thought only mothers knew, but maybe it's something they teach you in teacher school. By the time eight
bells ends, the boys are all sitting, mostly orderly, at the
back of the lifeboat.

They've left the seat directly in front of them empty.
It's the place Miss Gower asked them to vacate for me on
my first and last day as a student.

If I'd really left Lowell behind me, I'd sit down without
a second thought. I'd already have a reader out and open.

"Miss Deming, please help Milly and Maude prepare
an alphabet recitation." Miss Gower gestures to the little

redheads kicking each other at the front of the boat.

It takes me a moment to realize she's talking to me. I'm not a miss, though. Not like Nell or Flora. But perhaps it's right, if I'm going to invigilate, that I'm not just Jane.

Milly and Maude are four and five years old, and this is their first time in any sort of school. I try to lead them in saying the alphabet, but they keep mixing up the letters. They don't even know them all yet, and Milly is convinced x and y are the same letter. They also have that squirmy look Jer gets when he's made to stay inside too long.

Miss Gower's satchel is on the deck next to the lifeboat. I pull out a slate—cracked, but I can make do—and draw a clumsy picture of a cat.

"Who can tell me what this is?" I ask, and when both of them shout out the answer, I show them how to raise their hands and stand to recite and also to hold the boat-edge to keep their balance.

Milly and Maude like the idea of drawing pictures, so every time they say the alphabet once through properly, we play the guessing game. After a while it gets fun. Milly and Maude are how I picture Jer in a few years, old enough to understand jokes and do what they're told and not always be damp. The girls are talkative and sweet, even if they can't tell b from d and m from n. They're so excited to play the game that they concentrate on the alphabet and help each other when one forgets or makes a mistake.

Miss Gower comes over. "Whilst I listen to Milly and Maude recite, I would like you to help the boys with their longhand division." She gestures to the boys my age at the rear of the lifeboat—the Wakeman brothers, Charlie Pettys, and John Henry Wilson. They're elbowing one another like puppies in a crate and chortling like half-wits because Eugene Chase is crying over a single missed spelling word.

"Um . . ." What I'm umming around is that I struggle with ciphering. That I'm the last person who should invigilate it. "Ma'am, I . . ."

Miss Gower cocks her head like an owl, and that's enough to shut my mouth and send me to the bench in front of the boys. She takes the slate out of my hands and her brows go up when she sees the elephant. All I can do is hold out the rag I've been using as an eraser. She rubs away the picture without a word, then chalks a problem and hands the slate back.

826 divided by 3.

The boys and I follow the steps as well as I can remember, but each of us ends up with a number that can't possibly be right. Miss Gower shakes her head, brisk and firm, as each of us recites our answers.

I blink hard. I wish I were Nell. Her brother doesn't make her knit socks all day. He wouldn't care a jot if she wanted to come to school. She could quit invigilating the moment it became clear how badly she was doing. I'd take knuckles to the jaw now and then if that was the price.

"Since you're all struggling, I will demonstrate a problem for you." Miss Gower goes through each step, and when she gets to the carrying part, I flinch because I completely forgot to tell the boys to do that. "Now try again. Miss Deming, please sit down and contribute."

"But . . . but I'm not really . . ." *Helping. Useful. Ever-ever-ever going to get this.*

Miss Gower adjusts her spectacles. "You are not dismissed till your tasks for the day are completed. Your task for today is to practice longhand division with these boys until each of you presents a correct answer."

So I sit. I take the slate back. A dollar a week is money we're going to need badly.

Alf Wakeman gets the problem right first. Then John Henry, then Tudor, then Milner. At least I'm not last. Poor Charlie Pettys is, and he only manages at all because Alf kicks him twice in the shin to tell him the remainder.

Miss Gower nods briskly. "Acceptable, all around. Class is dismissed."

Acceptable. Miss Gower is never going to want me

back tomorrow. I sit on the edge of the lifeboat and put my head in my hands.

"Your tasks are complete," Miss Gower says, too loudly. "I will see you tomorrow at eight bells."

"Good, you're finally finished." Mrs. D is storming up the promenade deck, Jer fussing on her arm. "Honestly, I don't know what the matter is with him!"

Miss Gower said she'd see me tomorrow at eight bells. I can come back.

"Daney!" Jer reaches for me and Mrs. D gives him a little push when she hands him over. He grabs two handfuls of my hair and gives me a big, sticky kiss. "I pay Daney out."

"You want to play outside?" I repeat. "Didn't you tell your mama?"

Mrs. D groans. "Jane, you can't just let children do whatever they please. They must learn to sit still and do as they're told."

She must have tried to perch him next to her like a little doll all morning while she knitted. No wonder he's so happy to see me.

"Out! Pay Daney out."

I take Jer's hand. There are lots of things to look at on the promenade deck—girls flirting with officers, deckhands hauling lines, Nell and Flora in an alcove, giggling over something—but Mrs. D fixes me with a Look.

"There'll be time for everyone to enjoy themselves once we've landed," she says firmly. "Now, come along, both of you. Those socks won't make themselves."

7

RIO DE JANEIRO IS SOMETHING OUT OF A STORY-book.

Huge round stones bump out of the harbor like the back of a half-hidden sea serpent. Beyond, sheer brown-green cliffs jag against a stretch of busy, teeming buildings. It's damp-hot here, just like Lowell in the worst part of August, and I'm glad for my calico dress when the girls must all be sweltering in their wool and corsets.

Seattle probably has twice as many palm trees and even bluer water. Thank goodness I'll get to see Rio first, so I can do my gawking here and step off the boat in Washington Territory as if endless sandy beaches are old hand.

We anchor within easy sight of town. The captain

and the first mate go to the customs house by rowboat to announce our arrival. They haven't been back for a single turn of the glass before a crowd of girls starts gathering near the boat winch. Seeing the girls all together is a little frightening. Every last one looks like she stepped out of *Godey's Lady's Book* and sounds like she spent fifty years at finishing school.

If these girls are going to Washington Territory, though, we have to be more alike than we're not. There are no mills there, or town houses. We'll all start out the same.

Flora and I are sitting on a coil of rope while Jer plays with Hoss inside it. We're waiting for Nell and her brother. She promised he'd take us to see Rio's many sights. Mrs. D and Mrs. Pearson both said we were too young to go with the officers, but they agreed we could go with a *responsible adult* like Thad.

Who is now nowhere to be found.

"I hope she's all right," Flora murmurs.

Maybe we should go look for Nell. Only I don't want to find Thad before we find her.

"Stop! Stop this at once!" Mr. Mercer storms past us toward the boat winch, the wind blowing his hair every-whichway in stiff, oiled spines. "Just where do you think you're going?"

"Rio," Libbie Peebles replies in a voice that dares him

to challenge her. "The captain gave the officers leave to escort us around town. We're deciding who should go in which boat."

"I forbid it," Mr. Mercer says. "It's unseemly. Besides, this town is full of disease and ruffians. For your own safety, I must insist you all return to your rooms at once." He dusts his hands together like the matter is settled.

Libbie laughs and accepts Mr. Vane's hand. She swings up and over the side, and down the rope ladder toward the boat waiting below.

"Not your place to forbid, sir," Mr. Vane says with a smile, offering his hand to Ida May Barlow next.

Mr. Mercer storms away, muttering that the captain will hear of this. The girls and officers laugh rather unkindly. They do have a point. Surely, there can be nothing wrong with us taking in some fanciful sights we'll likely never see again.

Nell appears at the top of the portside ladder. Her jaw is clenched and she's hissing like a cat. "He's gone to Rio already. The engineers told me. He promised. The dirty blackguard."

Flora leaps up and hugs Nell. "It's all right, Nellie. It's not your fault."

"Yes it is! Now neither of you will get to see Rio, and it's on my head!"

I hug Nell too, and so does Jer, right around her legs. "Forget him. We'll get to Rio. Somehow."

One of the deckhands tells us that Mr. Conant, the newspaper reporter, plans to go to Rio in the next row-boat that returns to the *Continental*. "Hoping to catch up to the misses, he is," the deckhand adds with a sly grin.

Mr. Conant looks offended. "Certainly not. Merely recording details to prepare a dispatch for the *Times*."

"Then you wouldn't mind if we go with you?" I ask. "Me and Nell and Flora and Jer?"

Mr. Conant glances at the grinning deckhand, then smiles like he just lost a footrace. "I'd be delighted. As long as your parents all agree."

"Yes, sir," I reply. "They said we could go with a *responsible adult*."

On the ride across the harbor, Nell wipes her eyes. "I'm going to forget about that rascal. I'm going to have a good time in spite of him!"

Rio has the tiniest streets, and they are crowded with men and women and children, all different shades of brown and shiny as bronze. At the market, there are bowls made from clay and pretty rugs and strange flowers and fruits that are colors I can't name because I've never seen them. They're akin to colors I know—green, blue, pink—but nowhere near the same.

If Rio has so many new colors, I can't begin to imagine what awaits us in Washington Territory.

While we're waiting for the *Continental*'s oarsmen to row us back, I pick up a shell from the quayside. This was once a creature's home. Sturdy and smooth and colorful, now abandoned.

I press it into Flora's hands, then find one for Nell. They can think me childish if they want, but soon enough Flora will be standing by a beacon far from Seattle and surrounded by her family, and she'll have little enough to remember me by.

If we all have shells from Rio, it'll be a home we share.

Mrs. D returns to the *Continental* just after we do. She talked Mr. Mercer into taking her and several other widows to see the town, so she's in a bright mood. They're all a-chatter about climbing the huge mountain called Corcovado and seeing the lakes there, and even Mr. Mercer is smiling for a change.

I have high hopes for the rest of our week in Rio. The American consul and his wife have invited the girls to take tea, and there's a public fountain Mr. Conant says is quite educational if we want to see what Brazilians are like in their everyday lives.

Best of all, Mrs. Pearson says Flora might go with the girls on their next excursion as long as Nell goes with her.

She says she'll speak with Mrs. D about maybe letting me go too.

Only that's the night the officers from the other two American ships in Rio's harbor start arriving by the rowboatload. The captain stands by the winch and welcomes each with a hearty handshake while Mr. Mercer keeps repeating, "I forbid it. It's beyond unseemly. Girls, return to your rooms at once."

The girls all walk past him in their ribbons and lace, and there is laughter and chattering and plenty of strolling along the promenade deck.

Mr. Mercer finally gives up and grumbles his way below.

I don't have any ribbons or lace. Mostly I'm wandering around with Flora and Nell, and we're helping ourselves to the dainties put out for our guests. It doesn't hurt that Mr. Vane taught Jer to salute, and now he whips his little hand to his eyes every time he sees an officer's uniform, which everyone thinks is darling.

Mrs. D sweeps onto the promenade deck in her best and moves to join a circle of girls and officers chatting, but the girls keep a tight circle and give her only shoulders.

I elbow Flora, and we giggle at Mrs. D trying to pretend she's one of the misses instead of one of the missuses. Nell mutters something saucy I don't quite catch. Several nearby officers must overhear, because they grin.

When an officer from the *Shamokin* tries to include Mrs. D in the conversation, Julia Hood points to me stealing crackers with liver paste and Jer covered in sticky juice stains from earlier, and the men turn away without another look at Mrs. D.

For the rest of the evening.

Mrs. D spends what's left of our week in Rio in the ladies' cabin sullenly knitting socks and noticing every one of my dropped stitches and sighing over my color choices. I'm barely let out to invigilate or to use the necessary.

Mercifully, Mrs. D's black mood lifts the moment the last fawning officer steps into a rowboat back to his ship. That doesn't happen till our last night in Rio, though, and Nell and Flora both got to spend every evening on deck with them and all the tasty tidbits.

Just the two of them. Without me.

On the morning we're to leave Rio, the captain calls Nell into a corner of the saloon right before breakfast. She nods as he talks, but the color absolutely drains from her face. When he's done, she wobbles out of the room, all but falling against the wall.

By the time the porridge appears, the whole ship's company knows Nell's brother has abandoned her. Thad disappeared into the tiny streets of Rio and left behind a terse message with an oarsmen.

More trouble than she's worth.

I push my half-eaten breakfast away and go after her. Across the room Flora does the same. Mrs. D doesn't say a word. She even distracts Jer with an extra dollop of molasses so he doesn't see me leave.

We find Nell in Ladies, leaning heavily against a washtub. She slumps head-in-hands like her backbone went up in smoke.

"Oh, Nellie," Flora whispers.

Nell looks up. Her eyes are red, and she's trying to smile. "No, I'm all right. Really. I'm better off without that wretched brute. My passage is paid, and I hid some money from him. Seattle's the best place I can be. Really."

"You poor, poor dear," Flora murmurs.

"You want a cup of coffee?" I ask. "We have real coffee now. They grow it near Rio, did you know?"

Nell nods, so I go back to the saloon for a mug. The widows are all concern, wanting the gossip, but it's not mine to tell.

Libbie Peebles and Ida May Barlow sidle up to me while I'm pouring, and Libbie murmurs, "Mr. Mercer wants to appoint himself her guardian. As far as the girls are concerned, though, Nell is one of us now."

"Old Pap will find it hard to keep her under his thumb," Ida puts in cheerfully. "We'll see that she makes her own way in Seattle. Not his. So as far as you know, she's eighteen. Got that?"

Ida winks, and even though Nell has just gotten possibly the second-worst news of her life, she's no one's *poor dear*. Not with the family she's been fortunate enough to happen into.

8

LIBBIE PEEBLES AND IDA MAY BARLOW REALLY DO make Nell one of their own. Despite Mr. Mercer's vocal protests, Nell moves to their table in the saloon for meals, and every morning she and Flora disappear into the girls' secret room to play cards. In the evenings, they all appear from below in a big giggling crowd, chatting merrily in the music room before supper and sharing inside jokes in the corridors and taking turns playing Annie Miller's beloved piano that she paid a fortune to have brought on board. The one that made an empty room our music room.

Only now there is no *we*. There are friends-who-are-like-sisters and that girl with all the knitting calluses. There's them and there's me.

Just like Lowell.

One evening after supper I'm up on the hurricane deck watching the freezing, fog-strewn coast glide past when Nell appears at my elbow. She's bundled in a stylish cape that I've seen Ida wearing, and before I can ask how she's faring, she says, "Just tell the harpy it's part of your invigilating."

I frown. "What do you mean?"

"We want you to come play cards," Nell explains. "Flora and me. We've been talking. What if the harpy thinks the girls are teaching you to be a better invigilator when you're really learning the finer points of whist and eating gingerbread we're smuggling from the galley?" She says it offhand, like I wouldn't get in the worst kind of trouble if Mrs. D found out.

I've been knitting and feeling sorry for myself. Nell's been thinking up a way for me to join them.

"Tell her Miss Gower insists. Then the harpy can't say no." Nell winks. "Lots of girls down there are planning to teach. They can give you big teacher words to prove to the harpy you're really getting something out of it."

Nell leans against the rail, grinning and pink-cheeked from the wind. If she's still upset about her brother leaving, she's hiding it well. Or maybe she really is better off without him. She was saucy before; now she's all but glowing. Or perhaps she doesn't want anyone to treat her differently, so she's playacting like nothing has changed.

It's a hard playact to carry off when everything has changed.

"My stepmother would never credit such a thing," I reply, but already I want to believe she would, and that's a dangerous thing to want.

"Oh, come now, how often does the harpy talk to Miss Gower?" Nell raises her eyebrows. "Never, right?"

"Not if she doesn't have to," I admit. "Not even when Miss Gower pays my wages."

"There it is, then!" Nell slaps the rail as if that settles everything. "I'll meet you outside your stateroom tomorrow after you're done with school, and we'll go together. You won't know the secret knock."

"I should tell Miss Gower what I'm doing and ask her to go along with the story," I say. "She might understand. She considers my stepmother quite ridiculous."

"What if she won't? Miss Gower is awfully proper. She might not look kindly on you lying to an adult, even one she considers ridiculous."

Miss Gower does like things to be just so. She's also unfailingly truthful, even if it means saying things that aren't exactly polite. It was kind of her to give me an invigilator job, but if she truly wanted to help, she'd be giving me lessons in secret despite Mrs. D's mean-spiritedness.

Nell's the one who's really trying to help me. She doesn't have to either. She could just disappear into that secret card room with Flora and leave me penned up in Mrs. D's sock mill.

That means it's happening already. I'm only halfway to Washington Territory and already I'm someone a girl like Nell Stewart won't turn her back on.

So I straighten and tell her I'll be there. If I'm leaving Lowell behind, I have to shed every last bit of it.

Mrs. D frowns at me over her knitting needles. She's a little confused and a little suspicious, but she's not refusing out of hand.

"I'll be interviewing the girls who plan to teach in Washington Territory," I repeat, "so I can improve my invigilating. There's much I can learn from them."

Jer tromps past holding a length of ratline. His small friend, Jimmie Lincoln Pollard, is holding the other end, mooing and giggling and stomping small bare feet. Mrs. Pollard told me they've been playing farmer since mid-morning and haven't needed so much as a sharp word.

"Hmmm." Mrs. D's fingers never stop. "I don't suppose there's a pay rise."

I bite my lip. "No, ma'am."

"That Adelaide Gower." Mrs. D harrumphs. "I have

half a mind to tell her she can find a new invegetabler."

I figured Mrs. D would say something like that, so I open my carpetbag and show her the half-made sock and wad of yarn skewered with two needles nestled inside. "I plan to knit while I interview them. I don't need my fingers to listen."

Mrs. D squints at her pile of socks, then at Jer and Jimmie Lincoln absorbed in their game. "Very well. If there's nothing to be done for it."

I avoid giving a direct answer by making a show of packing a second hank of yarn, then I muss Jer's hair and hustle out of the ladies' cabin before Mrs. D can change her mind.

The room the girls have taken over is a disused storage berth, so it's large enough to hold twelve of us comfortably. They're sitting on the floor on army-looking blankets, with one girl per side like they're at proper tables. There are kerosene lanterns around the room and a row of portholes that let in daylight. I recognize everyone from the saloon and the promenade deck, but I let Flora introduce me.

They all seem as grown-up as Mrs. D, even though I know none is older than she is and many are not yet twenty. They all look like sturdy, bright-eyed future seamstresses and teachers, the toast of Rio and by now half of America, too, after Mr. Conant's dispatches of their adventures and demeanor.

This is what Seattle will be like with them in it. With *us* in it.

"Nell's told us about you," Ida says warmly. "Flora, too. It's a shame you're stuck minding your brother all the time. Come sit by me and I'll deal you in."

Ida and Flora and Julia Hood arrange themselves on the floor on the other edges of the blanket. Flora hands me a steaming mug of watered-down tea from a little paraffin burner on a table near a fire bucket sloshing with seawater. I lay my carpetbag aside to take it.

"Say, your stepmother's the snippy one, right?" Julia asks.

"The one with her nose in the air all the time, with the fancy ideas about marrying a banker?" asks Sarah Robinson.

"Ohhhh, her." Mary Anne Gifford rolls her eyes. "The one who's dead set on joining us everywhere we go. As if we wouldn't notice. As if the *officers* don't notice."

I sigh. "That's her."

Sarah puts a hand on mine. "Please tell her she's not like us and she's not fooling anyone. I don't like hearing the officers poke fun at her. It's beastly."

Mr. Vane and the rest are unfailingly polite to Mrs. D. At least, they are to her face.

People in Lowell were always nice to my face.

"Can we talk about something else?" I ask.

"Absolutely." Ida smiles and deals the cards. "Since you've come to discuss teaching, we'd best have a demonstration. Pay attention, Jane." She winks. "I just might ask you to recite."

They teach me how to hold cards. They teach me the different suits. They teach me the rules of whist. They are patient and cheerful, and no one mocks me when I mistake spades for clubs or play out of turn.

If this were school, I'd swear my mind was getting broader.

In whist, you win by matching suits and taking tricks. You have to be sneaky sometimes and play a lower card to fool your opponent into thinking it's your highest one. You have to make a plan that doesn't seem to go anywhere when you're making it, but by the end of the hand, things turn out just the way you wanted.

Whist is mostly about being patient, especially when you don't see anything good come of what you're doing right away. Especially when you lose a lot at the beginning. When you lose at the beginning, mostly you're setting up to win at the end.

9

A WEEK AFTER WE ROUND CAPE HORN, THE SHIP awakens to a sky that's blue and glorious. Instead of playing whist, we all go out on the promenade deck to soak up some sun. Mr. Conant is already there, sketching the shoreline. We're nearing Lota, a little town in Chile where we'll take on coal and spend a few days like we did in Rio.

One of the deckhands starts shouting, and sure enough, there are sails in the distance.

"Maybe she'll be an American man-o'-war," Nell muses. "I wouldn't mind another shipful of officers."

"Her flag is yellow and red," I reply. "Not ours. Why is there smoke coming from her?"

Mr. Conant barely glances over his reporter pad.

"She's flying Spanish colors, my dear, and what you're seeing is a smoke signal."

"It's like a pillar. Are they all right?"

"What the devil?" He fumbles the pad as he whips a hand to his eyes. "Damnation. Her gunports are all open!"

There's a faint, faraway *crack*, then a rush-whistle that gets louder by the moment until something big and hard hits the water just off the bow and sends up a menacing spray.

I gape at Mr. Conant. "Are they *firing* on us? Was that a *cannonball?*"

"Mama," Flora whispers, and she's off like a rabbit toward the starboard ladder.

"You girls should go below too." Mr. Conant starts scribbling on his reporter pad.

Ida grabs Julia and Sarah, and they rush after the others. Nell holds the rail with one hand and my forearm with the other, and she grips hard. There's no way I'm leaving her here alone.

Another faraway *crack*, then a different sound—*shink-shink-shink*—and two cannonballs chained together come rattling along the port side *right under me*.

"W-why are the Spanish firing on us?" I manage. "We're not at war with them."

"No," Mr. Conant replies, still writing furiously, "but

they are at war with Chile. They must think we're trying to run the blockade and bring supplies through to the Chileans."

There was a blockade during the secession war. Federal ships stopped rebel ships from getting any cotton or messages out, and anyone from getting food and medicine to the rebels. Plenty of vessels got sunk trying to sneak past, often with all hands lost.

The Spanish man-o'-war is closer now, and our deckhands are reefing the sails. We're slowing down, but at least there are no more cannonballs.

Mr. Conant curses. "Stay close, girls. We're about to be boarded."

Nell turns to me and holds up a fist. "If you have to hit a sailor, use your knuckles and aim for his windpipe. Like this. My brother showed me. Guess he was useful for something."

I make a fist like Nell's. I'm not sorry I didn't hide belowdecks with the others. If something bad is going to happen, I want to see it coming.

Spanish sailors swarm the *Continental*. They are nothing like our deckhands. They're a hard lot, all pistols and gap-teeth and raggedy trousers, and they shove and manhandle anyone foolhardy enough to get in their way.

Half a dozen widows, led by Mrs. D, start shrieking

from where they've barricaded themselves in the ladies' cabin. She has a voice like a cat with a bellyache and I would know it anywhere.

Mr. Conant shoves his reporter pad into his coat pocket and holds his hands up in surrender. I do the same, and several Spanish sailors laugh at me. Nell presses her shoulder against mine, her fist at her side. She looks fierce and sturdy, like I wish I felt.

The older girls are openly weeping near the foremast. They don't ever come to whist, so I know them only by name, but the way they're carrying on, you'd think the Spanish are roasting them alive. Mr. Mercer is trying to comfort them, since our captain told him to hush his mouth and say nothing to the Spanish commander if he knew what was good for him.

A Spanish officer spends a long time talking to our captain and reviewing the ship's papers. The captain even has Nell and Ida and Libbie meet the officer to prove we're a passenger ship full of seamstresses and schoolteachers.

The officer finally accepts that we ran the blockade purely by mischance and really aren't helping the Chileans. Then he gives us leave to go to Lota to get coal and water, but he follows us all the way with his gunports open.

Mr. Vane is given the task of accounting for every person on the *Continental* and assuring them we are not prisoners of the Spanish Crown. Lots of people hid in their staterooms, and the Wakeman boys were down in the boiler room with the three engineers, ready with big, oily wrenches to club any Spaniards who tried to seize it.

By suppertime, the girls are all making jokes and laughing about the *misunderstanding*. They're saying things like *The newspapers will refuse to print a tale this tall* and *Does this mean we're combat veterans?* Ida tells the others how Nell was the picture of brass—chin up, eyes steady, even though the Spanish officer was hulking over them like an ogre.

Nell, happily squeezed between Libbie and Julia, tells everyone she'd never have had such brass without me there at her shoulder. The card-room girls all lift their glasses of ship's beer and toast me from their table across the saloon.

I toast them in return with my tea, then I make a fist under the table. I don't ever want to hit anyone, but I like knowing that I could if I have to.

Every other Saturday, Miss Gower hands Mrs. D a two-dollar bill for my wages. She always does it in the saloon just before a meal so I can see her do it.

Each time, I hold my breath. Each time, Mrs. D smiles that pointy smile and holds her hand out, and Miss Gower makes a show of letting the money flutter onto her palm.

Neither of them ever says a word.

The girls have all sworn themselves to secrecy. They're even helping me make socks; whoever is sitting out a hand knits a few rows or binds off or turns a heel.

Nell swears I could make my fortune in a San Francisco card room, because she can never tell when I'm bluffing. Must be all those years of saying *yes, ma'am* to Mrs. D when I had Opinions I knew better than to share.

Ida invents terms like *rational schoolroom* and *curriculum learning* for me to repeat back to Mrs. D each night at supper.

While we're on the Galápagos Islands, Flora and I catch Mr. Conant, the reporter, spying on the older girls as they splash in an inlet without their shoes and stockings. He swears he was merely collecting shells and happened upon them by accident, but he gives us each a thumb-sized glass bead from Rio after we promise not to tell. Flora stitches hers onto her reticule, but I slip mine in my pocket alongside my lucky hopscotch stone.

In less than a month we'll arrive in Washington Territory, and I'm about as far from Lowell as a girl like me can get.

I'm finally ready to arrive.

☙ ☙ ☙

The whole ship's company cheers when the captain announces we've reached San Francisco, but it takes us half a day to even get near the city. The strait leading into the bay is perilous to navigate, so the *Continental* must follow a pilot. Mr. Vane spends a whole day in a rowboat finding a pilot who charges a rate that isn't completely ruinous.

San Francisco itself is unsightly, like a smear of mud you'd scrape off your shoe. Mr. Conant explains there was an earthquake here not a year ago and people are still rebuilding from it. To say nothing of the fires that keep leveling a town made mostly of shacks and canvas.

I'm glad we're not staying long.

We anchor late, so no one goes into town. Mr. Mercer and the captain are both absent from supper. The widows all have Opinions on what might be going on, but I just eat two helpings of beans and work out how to ask Mrs. D if I might join Flora and Nell and Mrs. Pearson on the first rowboat trip into San Francisco tomorrow.

At breakfast the captain rises from his place at the front table. "Your attention, please! By eight bells of the forenoon watch—that's twelve noon to you landsmen— all passengers are to gather with their belongings on the promenade deck. You will be taken to Folsom Wharf by rowboat and deposited there along with your baggage."

"We're not disembarking here," Mrs. Pearson says, and several others loudly agree. "We're bound for Washington Territory. We've all paid our passage."

The captain's eyes narrow. "You've paid your passage to San Francisco. This ship goes no further. I've had it with Asa Mercer and his endless parade of folly."

I suck in a harsh, sudden breath that makes Jer turn worried eyes up at me, porridge all over his face and front.

"Now, wait just a blessed minute!" Mrs. Grinold rises with her fists tight, as if she took lessons from Nell. "Mr. Mercer would never allow this. He made us a promise."

Mr. Mercer stands up. He's not sitting at the captain's table anymore, and he looks like he hasn't slept since Rio. "Everything is in hand. Please do as the captain says, and when you land, proceed to either the Fremont House Hotel or the International Hotel. It might be a few days, but I will arrange the necessary transportation to Seattle. If you're not in one of those hotels, I can't promise I'll be able to find you with particulars."

All around me, grown-ups are muttering, and some are using bad words.

"I never believed the papers when they said those awful things about him. Guess I should have."

"I'm not going another step. At least San Francisco has some semblance of civilization. If we keep following this madman, who *knows* where we might end up."

"Those girls. Poor dears."

No. He promised. Mr. Mercer said there'd be particulars. He might be a fuss-and-feathers dandy who folds his drawers, but he's not a scoundrel.

"Jane, finish your breakfast and then go pack our trunk," Mrs. D says quietly. "Take Jer with you. Miss Gower won't expect you today."

Mrs. D doesn't even wait for a *yes, ma'am*. She stands up and straightens her hat and plows toward the crowd of women surrounding Mr. Mercer and stabbing angry fingers at him.

I kind of want to join her.

Jer starts crying. He's usually good-natured, but he can tell something's wrong. I have to carry him flailing all the way down to the stateroom and leave him sobbing on the bottom bunk while I pack.

I kind of want to join him, too.

Once the trunk's all ready, I climb up to my top bunk and collect my own carpetbag. I know I should comfort Jer, but I pull out Mr. Mercer's pamphlet with all my improvements and press it to my cheek for a long, long moment before I do.

10

FOLSOM WHARF IS CROWDED WITH MEN. NOT
gentlemen, either. These men are tattered and dirty, like
the beggars back in Lowell who'd come around in what
was left of their army uniforms, barefoot, bareheaded, and
smelling like a privy in July. They are yelling things that
actually make Mrs. D put her hands over my ears.

I hold Jer tight so he doesn't fall out of the rowboat
trying to get the seagulls that are winging everywhere.
Miss Gower mutters that the whole scene is *sordid* while
holding her reticule like a club.

There are also policemen with cudgels on the wharf.
They beat and menace the crowd enough that the sailor
at the oars can guide our boat to the dock. Mr. Vane steps
out of the rowboat, takes one look at the blur of ruffians

and flashing cudgels, and says he'll accompany us to the hotel.

The way is uphill, and we have to walk every step of it—no carriages or cabmen here—over roads more mud than dirt and littered with horse apples. There's a crowd of men the whole way as if we're some sort of parade, and there are mutters of *schoolma'ams* and *tender maidens* and something about *a cargo of petticoats* that makes me scowl.

My friends are not cargo. They are more than their undergarments.

The International Hotel is a white-painted building set into a hillside. There are more men spread in two wide aprons on either side of the hotel door, pushing and jostling. They're bushy and uncombed, and they wear blue work trousers and clodhopper boots like it's a uniform.

"Walk past them," Mr. Vane says through his teeth. "They won't hurt you."

They don't seem to mean us harm, though. They keep shouting things like *Marry me!* and *I'm worth a thousand in gold!*

As if that will tempt us when we're bound for the Queen City of King County.

Girls arrive in twos and threes, escorted by officers from the ship, and we all wait in the parlor for Mr. Mercer's particulars. Nell arrives with Ida and Sarah, and we crowd into a window seat while Ida breathlessly relates the latest rumors about Mr. Mercer, and Jer strings up Hoss with Nell's ribbons.

Washington Territory is a dismal place where it does nothing but rain! Beardy faces crowd the windows, and big, square hands wave frantically for our attention. *Stay here in California where you'll see the sun every day!*

It's a low trick, making up stories to try to get us to stay. It's a good thing I've read Mr. Mercer's pamphlet back to front, so I can see through their pitiful lies.

An anxious week later Mr. Mercer comes by the hotel and gives us particulars. Two sailing vessels will be leaving for Washington Territory over the next several days. Each of them will take half the passengers to Port Townsend, and from there, lumber schooners will take us in dozens to Seattle.

The captains of the *Scotland* and the *Huntsville* have been well compensated to assist all passengers in reaching Seattle without incident, regardless of whether Mr. Mercer is present on board to direct them. We are to do as the captains bid us and absolutely not worry about a thing.

Nell harrumphs at that part, but she is not one of the three dozen of the ship's company who have decided to stay in San Francisco. Bad enough that Flora will soon be away to her lighthouse. Losing Nell to San Francisco would have been like Lowell all over again.

On the day before the first vessel departs, Nell and Flora arrange a social in the parlor of the International Hotel. Mrs. D says I might go, and Mrs. Pollard is happy for Jer to play with Jimmie Lincoln all afternoon.

The girls gather around Annie Miller's piano, which was painstakingly hauled by long-suffering deckhands all the way to the hotel. Nell and Flora are sipping lemonade near the window. They're both leaving tomorrow on the *Scotland*, and even though I'll see Nell again in Seattle, Flora will be going to her lighthouse straight from Port Townsend.

I'll probably never see her again.

". . . Georgie tells me Whidbey Island is nothing like Seattle," Flora is saying, "except for the Indians, and—"

"Indians?" I repeat.

Back in Lowell, and New York, too, newspapers were full of stories of the wars with Indians out on the plains where the covered wagons were trying to cross.

"Well, yes," Flora replies, like I'm missing something obvious. "Indians live around Seattle, lots of them, even though they're supposed to be on reservations. That's what the big treaty was about. But on the reservations there's nothing for them to do, and they go hungry. There's more than enough work to go around in Seattle for white people and Indians both. Not everyone is happy about it, but that's the way it is."

Flora goes on about what Indians near Puget Sound are like, how they fish and gather berries and paddle canoes, and how I shouldn't be afraid.

It hadn't occurred to me to be afraid. Mostly, I'm curious, because there's not a word about Indians in Mr. Mercer's pamphlet.

The social lasts till suppertime. No one wants to be the first to leave the parlor. It's only when the hotel-keeper stands in the doorway and repeatedly clears his throat that we hug and weep and straggle out in ones and twos.

Soon it's only me and Flora and Nell.

"I'll write," Flora whispers.

Nell nods briskly as she scrubs at her eyes, but I can't bring myself to promise the same. Not if it might make a liar of me. I have seven blank pages at the end of the little book Miss Bradley made for me and a stumpy pencil Mr. Conant had no use for. Once those are used up, I can't be sure I'll be able to get more.

It hurt when my Lowell friends stopped coming around, but Jer and the housekeeping made me so busy and tired that I just looked up one day and they were gone. I never had to say good-bye for good. I never had to watch them walk away.

Only days later Mrs. D, Jer, and I are back on Folsom Wharf along with twenty other passengers. There's no attempt at order. No hand-wringing about propriety. We're told to be on the wharf at barely-dawn with our baggage and embark on the *Huntsville*.

On our way out of the International we pass Mr. Mercer signing over Annie Miller's piano to the hotel owner, swearing front to back it's a down payment on the whole boarding bill.

The *Huntsville* is a sailing ship, not a steamship, and there are no necessaries or staterooms. There's only an open space beneath the deck, where we're meant to eat and bed down and do our business. The deckhands are surly and weathered and don't wink and chuck my chin when I ask questions like *What beam is the wind off?*

Still, we're almost to Washington Territory. The captain says it won't be more than three weeks till we get to Port Townsend. Maybe less if the weather helps. Then only a week to Seattle!

The first few days are pretty and blue, then the sky turns a dull gunmetal gray and stays that way. I improve the section on Climate in Mr. Mercer's pamphlet with a clumsy drawing of a palm tree like I saw in Rio.

The girls all went on the first vessel, so there's not much to occupy myself with. In Mr. Mercer's mind, Miss Gower counts as a girl, so she isn't here to hold a school. Not that there's any room for it on the *Huntsville*. Mostly, I watch for the moment when the needly trees start becoming palm trees, but instead they fade into the fog, and then there's nothing to see but fog.

For three days it rains. Not a playful, light tropical rain, but a heavy, drenchy rain that sheets down and soaks right through the wool traveling cloak I'm now glad Mrs. D didn't unravel for the yarn.

I show Jer how to knit socks, but he's too little to follow along. So I try to teach him and Jimmie Lincoln to play hopscotch instead, only the roll of the ship sends our markers tumbling, and the rain washes away the squares I chalk on the deck, and they can never remember to keep one foot in the air.

The *Huntsville* arrives at Port Townsend one damp morning before dawn, and by the evening tide the passengers are divided into two smaller groups and outbound for Seattle on lumber schooners, just as Mr. Mercer said we'd be. The schooners are empty of goods, as they intend to pick up timber in Seattle for the Port Townsend mills, so the captain figures on a quick run down Puget Sound. I overhear the dockside gangers saying how the *cargo of petticoats* departed for Seattle two days earlier, and while it still irks me to hear my friends talked about in such a way, it won't be long before we're all together again.

I reread Mr. Mercer's pamphlet at least once a day, cover to cover, along with all my improvements. We're in Washington Territory now, and once we land, there'll be plenty of room for Jer to run and schoolhouses on every corner and a nice, rich banker for Mrs. D to marry. We'll live in a big house made of new-cut boards and eat hot, tasty food at every meal and my friends will be around the corner and down the road and across town. I'll visit someone's house every day after school and we'll play whist for hours.

It's all just through the fog. It's all there, even if I can't see it.

I frown at the sailor and repeat, "That's Seattle."

"Oh aye, m'girl." He points again through the drizzle at the scattering of unremarkable white buildings cluttered along a bay like they're trying to escape the solid wall of timber rising behind them.

I can't see a bank.

I can't see a church.

I can't see anything that might resemble a school.

We're heading toward a wharf that's connected to a long, muddy track that stretches up and up and disappears into the timber beyond. To the left is a lumber mill where men wrestle big logs up a chute from the water into the cutting area. Some of the workers are brown men with their sleeves rolled up and their hair about their shoulders. Or rather they are bronze, like the people in Rio. They must be Indians.

Beyond the millhands there's no one on the wharf. No crowds of eligible gentlemen pushing and fighting for a look at us. Not even any barefoot miners hollering ugly things like in San Francisco.

"This can't be Seattle," I tell the sailor, as if he could snap his fingers and make it right. Or more like he'd grin and *pshaw* me and we'd keep sailing and soon enough find that busy, bustling town from the pamphlet. The one that hums with Trade and Industry and other chapter headings.

Instead, he shrugs. "What'd you expect?"

Mrs. D comes up from below. She's wearing her Sunday dress, and Jer's in a clean shirt and britches. She's already smiling that pretty-headtilt smile.

The water here is deep enough to hold up a ship, so we won't need to fool about with rowboats. The sailors hail the men on the wharf. Several millhands come and stand ready to catch the lines the sailors hold in massive coils.

Mrs. D cranes her neck, peering at the dock like I did a few minutes ago. Like I could change it just by rubbing my eyes.

The men on the dock wind the lines around the posts while the captain calls *drop anchor*.

The wharf stretches in front of us, crooked and splintering. It ends where a slope of weed-strewn gravel makes a sort-of beach. Where the wharf turns into the road, there's nothing but mud.

There's no sand. No blue water. Not a palm tree in sight.

We're here.

And there has to be some mistake.

11

THE TEN OF US STAND UNCERTAINLY ON THE wharf while sailors pile our baggage at our feet. I'm holding Jer, because he refuses to stand on his own. Mrs. D keeps peering at the millworkers like they'll part somehow and reveal her banker. She fidgets with the cameo at her collar, the lace around her cuffs. Already her flouncy hem is dingy just from the boards of the wharf.

Three men clomp out of the mill. They're wearing shirts made of red flannel and the sort of heavy blue work trousers the miners wore in San Francisco.

"You're Mercer's, right?" one demands.

I draw a sharp breath. We might owe Mr. Mercer some money, but this country just finished fighting a whole war over whether anyone could own another person.

Mrs. Horton clears her throat indignantly. "I should think not. We're part of the Mercer emigration expedition, yes, but—"

"You wanna get married?"

"Well—" Mrs. Horton makes an awkward gesture. "I—might. But—"

"He said he was bringing us wives," the beardiest one cuts in. "I paid good money."

This can't be right. It *can't* be. Mr. Mercer brought us here because we have broad minds and sturdy constitutions and we'll enrich the territory with our industriousness and thrift and good breeding. He said as much, more times than I can count.

Mrs. Horton lifts her chin. "I'll only marry if a man's got gold in his pockets and one foot in the grave."

"Told you," the first says to the others, and all three of them huff in disgust and grumble off toward a white building on the other side of the wharf.

Mrs. D looks like she might faint right here on the boards. "They were supposed to meet us on the pier. Dozens of them. Gentlemen. I was going to . . ."

"Ma'am?" I tug Mrs. D's puffy sleeve. "Should we find a hotel? Jer's getting hungry."

Also, I'd like to get well clear of those three men and any others like them.

There's a house across from the mill. It's made of proper boards and it's got windows and curtains and a big porch. A man steps out dressed in a suit that's New York–fancy. Mrs. D's eyes light up, even though he's old enough to be my grandfather. He introduces himself as Mr. Yesler and welcomes us to Seattle. The house is his, and so are the mill and the wharf and the land we're standing on.

"The others are at the Occidental Hotel," Mr. Yesler says. "Just yonder. Mrs. Yesler is already there. She's taken it upon herself to make sure the girls have everything they need. Here, I'll walk with you there."

Mrs. D's silly-face goes back to normal. The way he says *Mrs. Yesler* makes me think it's not something he'd ordinarily put into a conversation, but he's learned to very recently.

"We'll have to beg your pardon for the lukewarm welcome," Mr. Yesler goes on. "You're the second schooner to arrive today from Port Townsend with passengers from the expedition. We expected Mr. Mercer's girls back in January, so when no one arrived for month after month, we figured the whole thing had fallen through."

"We didn't even sail till January," I tell him.

"That's what the others said." Mr. Yesler sounds annoyed, like our not arriving till summer put him out personally.

Away from the wharf, the town feels bigger. There

are three streets that cross the mill road, but because of the shape of the bay they crook when they cross, like the bend in an elbow. We pass a big log building and smaller buildings made of milled boards. The first is the mill's cookhouse, the next few are stores. There are other buildings too, but those don't have signs and Mr. Yesler forgets to tell us what they're for.

Everything feels huddled by the water. Almost as if the wall of timber is a fat lady you're sharing a settee with, and her large rear end is pushing you to the very edge.

The Occidental Hotel is white and has lots of windows and a big porch like Mr. Yesler's. It sits in a triangle made of three streets, one of which is so muddy there's a bridge over it.

Come to think on it, there's no chapter in the pamphlet about roads.

"Hungeeeeeey, Daneeeeeey," Jer whines.

"Of course the gentlemen wouldn't be at the wharf." Mrs. D is talking, but I don't think she's talking to me. "They'd be at the hotel. Waiting for us where there's a teaspoon of civilization."

She starts biting her lips red and straightening her hat.

Five steps inside the Occidental, Mrs. D stops in her tracks and I bump into her.

The parlor is packed with men.

Young, old, everywhere in between. They're in raggedy clothes, mostly, but a few wear suits that are threadbare at the elbows and hopelessly out of fashion. Their beards look like blackberry thickets, bushy and unkempt.

To a man, they stand up the moment Mrs. D appears in the foyer.

I cover Jer's ears the best I can with one hand, but they don't start yelling vulgar things like the men did in San Francisco. They don't say a single word. If anything, they act like someone just punched them in the windpipe and they're recovering their wits.

"Stand here, Jane," Mrs. D hisses. "Don't move."

She puts her chin in the air and glides over to the registry desk like a queen in a fairy tale.

"Daneeeeeey, hungeeeeeeey!"

One of the beardy men steps toward us. He's got wispy brownish hair and a belly like a pillow stuffed under his red flannel shirt. He's holding out something that looks like a shriveled-up piece of shoe leather.

"You like jerky, son?"

Jer takes the strip and peers at it.

"You eat it." He produces his own piece of shoe leather jerky and bites down. "Mmmmm."

Jer gnaws once—twice—on the jerky. He frowns, then offers it back. "Not for eat."

"I'm real sorry, sir," I say, but the burly man only laughs and pockets the jerky.

"He's probably right. I'm not sure bachelor rations count as food."

Mrs. D rushes past me, head down. She's breathing like a racehorse just across the finish line, and she's not heading toward the dining room where there are voices and laughter and the clink of cutlery.

"Thanks anyway," I reply, and the man holds his jerky up in salute.

"Can we eat?" Jer asks in a forlorn voice.

I'm hungry too, and delicious smells are coming from the Occidental's dining room. Roasted meat. Buttery bread. *Pie*.

"Let's go find your mama," I tell him. "Then we'll all eat together."

"Mama," Jer agrees, so I hoist him higher and venture after Mrs. D. A door slams at the end of a dim corridor. There's a fancy wooden sign on it that says LADIES ONLY. I tap on the door, and when she doesn't answer, I peek in.

Mrs. D is lying on a faded pink fainting couch, facing the wall. She isn't crying, but she isn't moving, either.

"Mama?" Jer climbs on the couch next to her. "Mama? Up."

"Ma'am?" I clear my throat. "Are you feeling all right?"

She laughs, high and shrill. "Four thousand miles, children. Four *thousand* miles. There's not one gentleman to be had, not one. Just . . . men."

"Maybe they're nice," I say.

"Nice?" Mrs. D whips around, eyes terrifying. "Do you know what they do? They're loggingmen. Miners. This is as clean as they've been in a year! Half of them don't even have a pot to piss in, much less a roof to keep us all under. That snake in the grass Asa Mercer promised me . . . I'm going to kill him with my bare hands."

Jer starts snuffly-crying, slides off the couch, and grabs me around the legs. I pick him up and sway aimlessly.

We came this whole way so Mrs. D could get married. It was all she wanted, to get married and keep house. Now she can. She's got her pick. Every single man in that parlor would trip over himself to make her smile.

"Perhaps all the bankers are busy today," I say, and when she makes this little strangled noise, I hold Jer tighter. I can *yes ma'am* Mrs. D like a champion when she's raging or annoyed. A Mrs. D falling to pieces like Jer when he needs a nap—my throat is closing just being near her.

So I ask if Jer and I can go eat, because at least that will solve one of our problems.

She mumbles something that might be *I don't care*. I tug out my handkerchief and wipe away the last of Jer's tears. "C'mon, let's go see what's for supper."

"Hoss," Jer mumbles, so I fish the toy out of my carpet-bag and hand it to him. Even though it's pointy and wooden, he hugs it close.

As we pass the registry desk, Mrs. Grinold comes down the stairs. I tell her where Mrs. D is, and ask if she'd go look in on her. Mrs. Grinold is the closest thing Mrs. D has to a friend-who's-like-a-sister, and right now she needs all the family she can get.

Mrs. Pollard takes one look at me standing in the doorway of the Occidental's dining room and pulls Jer out of my arms and plops him down next to Jimmie Lincoln. Jer is so delighted to see his small friend from the *Continental* that he forgets why he's crying and helps himself to some of Jimmie's eggs.

When Jer stops crying, I feel less like I might start.

Mrs. D might have had a shock, but she isn't being fair. We've barely seen any of Seattle, and already she's judging it too harshly, and Mr. Mercer, too. Sure, there seem to be fewer buildings than I pictured. More mud, too, and a lot more stumps and buildings on stilts and a strange set of wooden pipes on stilts too. And no side-walks to speak of.

Mrs. Grinold will talk some sense into her. Tomorrow

we can take a proper tour of the town. It'll be like stepping into the pamphlet. We'll find the school and the bank, and Mrs. D can flirt her head off at whatever poor man is behind the counter while I figure out when to expect the school bell.

"Miss Deming. It's a pleasure to see you've arrived none the worse for wear."

Miss Gower appears beside me, buttoned-up prim and adjusting her spectacles and using big words at me. Out of habit I straighten, even though I kind of want to hug her as if she were Flora or Nell.

"You too!" I squeal. Then I add, because it's Miss Gower, "Ma'am."

"I'm delighted I'm able to wish you well before I leave."

"You—you're leaving?" Not her as well. "You can't."

"Yes." She takes my arm and leads me away from Jer and Jimmie Lincoln fighting over a biscuit. "I've been offered a school in Olympia. The next steamer leaves the day after tomorrow."

"I want to keep invigilating for you," I protest. "You were going to be the Old Maid of the Territory."

"Olympia is still in the territory. It's unfortunate our geography lessons were so limited."

"I thought we'd all be together," I say in a faint voice. "Here. In Seattle."

Miss Gower turns me by the shoulders to look out on the Occidental's dining room. "You are. You girls are all here, but for a few weary enough to stay in California or drawn to loved ones elsewhere. You are all here together."

The room is full of familiar faces. Girls I played whist with. Girls I sang with beside Annie Miller's poor pawned piano. My fellow combat veterans.

My friends are here on their own, though. No mothers or stepmothers or brothers to tell them to knit socks or mind their manners. They laughed at Mr. Mercer when he tried to play at Father. Any one of my friends could have marched into Miss Gower's lifeboat and picked up a slate without asking anyone's permission.

"I need you, too," I reply.

Miss Gower gives that almost-smile. "I doubt you do. After all, you admirably managed to assign yourself additional tasks all on your own account."

"You—you *knew?*"

"The *Continental* wasn't that large a vessel. Once your ruse came to my attention, I did not dissuade anyone of its origin. I saw no reason to empower those who decide matters on your behalf from a place of ignorance." Miss Gower's brows flutter. "I so dislike anyone who insists on preserving ignorance."

She means Mrs. D. She didn't like Mrs. D making me knit socks and mind Jer instead of going to school, where I could broaden my mind and keep my promise to Papa.

Miss Bradley said *good luck*. Miss Gower did what she could to help, even if that was only giving me a job invigilating.

"Now I really don't want you to go," I whisper.

Miss Gower fidgets with her spectacles. "Seattle has become a village of schoolteachers. If you continue to learn everything you can from them, you will prevail."

"*Prevail*. Is that Latin too?" I don't care, not really, but it will keep her here and talking that much longer.

"It is," Miss Gower replies with that delightful raised eyebrow I just can't seem to imitate. "From *valēre, to be worth*, and *prae, because of*. Those who pursue knowledge for its own sake *because it's worth something*."

All at once I see what Miss Gower is trying to big-word at me. Here in Seattle, I can likely go back to school. Mrs. D was ready to let me sit for lessons in the lifeboat until she learned who was in charge of them. If Miss Gower's not the teacher anymore, Mrs. D will have less trouble sending me to recite for Julia or Ida or whatever miss is holding class here right now.

Which is nice and all, but none of my friends approached Mrs. D in the saloon that morning and

Latined me a position in her lifeboat school for a dollar a week.

Miss Gower squeezes my hand and turns to go. She's still not the sort of person you hug without warning, but I can't help myself. I throw my arms around her tight. I don't expect her to hug me back, but she pulls me close and pats my shoulders just like Mama used to all those years ago.

JER IS STILL HAPPY EATING WITH JIMMIE LINCOLN, and Mrs. Pollard is content to keep him, so I join Nell and Ida and Julia Hood for supper.

The girls have all been here for days, so they've already met Seattle's leading citizens and seen the parts of town those citizens want seen. Nell's grin is devilish when she reveals that the buildings without signs I saw on my way to the hotel are dens of vice.

That certainly wasn't in the pamphlet. Nell must be mistaken. Seattle isn't San Francisco by a mile and change.

"Your schooner is the last of us to arrive," Ida says as the plates are cleared. "We thought maybe you'd decided to settle elsewhere."

That must be why so few people were on the wharf to greet us. Our little vessel out of Port Townsend was a boatload of widows, and all the girls came ahead of us. The girls were who everyone was waiting for. Not a passel of widows trailing children.

"I'm glad you didn't, though," Julia puts in.

"They expected hundreds of us, did you know?" Nell says. "They had everything ready for us back in January. People volunteered to let us sleep on their floors in bed-rolls."

"They're mad as anything that they did all this work and gathered so many supplies and had a reception planned—and we never showed!" Ida laughs and shakes her head.

"Are they still willing?" I ask, because if we don't have to pay for a hotel, my invigilating money will go a lot further.

"Ask Mrs. Yesler," Nell replies. "She got each of us a place to board. The Carrs couldn't be more wonderful. Although I thought the harpy meant to marry right away. A banker." She's teasing, and I smile because I've missed Nell sorely, and teasing Mrs. D is always an amusing sport. My heart's not in it today, though.

"I suppose I should go find Mrs. Yesler," I say, but Nell is pulling a familiar deck of cards from her reticule.

"I'm sure it's already handled," Nell says. "Seattle ladies are absolutely delightful. Who's ready to lose badly at whist?"

Julia makes a show of cracking her knuckles, and Ida pours everyone another cup of tea.

So I sit. I let things be handled and just play cards with my friends.

Mrs. Pollard brings Jer when she has to take Jimmie Lincoln out back to wash the eggs out of his hair. I start to get up, but Ida says, "Don't you dare. We need a fourth."

So Jer sits on my lap, and I let him put down hearts and spades as I point to them. He giggles when the girls pronounce him ready for the card rooms of San Francisco.

"All right, you lot," the hotel owner says.

I look up, but he's not talking to us. He's facing the men still sitting in the parlor with their hands folded and their big boots awkward under fancy chairs.

"Either pay for a room or go elsewhere," the owner goes on. "The stable's half-price."

The bachelors don't argue or protest or threaten. They simply file out through the dining room, staying close to the wall opposite. A few glance our way, but most face forward and button their coats against the downpour echoing on the roof.

Like this is something they do every night.

"You won't believe this," Ida says in a low voice as she fans out her cards, "but Mr. Mercer took three hundred dollars from every single one of them."

I don't want to believe that, but after what happened on the wharf, I think I have to.

"I was on the first schooner that arrived from Port Townsend." Nell smirks. "There were those poor fools on the beach, fresh from their homesteads in grubby trousers and torn greatcoats, waiting to go straight to the preacher. You should have seen their faces when we all walked past them to the hotel. I thought they'd lynch Old Pap on the nearest tree!"

"They can't make us marry them, can they?" Julia whispers.

Ida and Nell both make disparaging noises, and Julia's cheeks go pink. Mine, too, probably, because three hundred dollars is an unfathomable lot of money, and lynching is serious business.

"Mrs. Carr told me to take all the time I needed to make wise decisions." Nell shifts cards in her hand. "I'm not to feel hurried or unwelcome in her home."

"I feel sorry for them," I say. "Mr. Mercer led them to believe one thing, but they ended up with something completely different."

Maybe he gave them a different pamphlet. *Reflections Upon Your East Coast Bride.*

"Me too, a little," Nell replies, "but just because they gave Asa Mercer money doesn't mean I'm in any hurry to *marry* one of them. He's the one who made promises, not me."

"Mr. Mercer certainly didn't mention this fact when I asked him for particulars back in New York," Ida adds.

Useful employment. That's what Mr. Mercer told Mrs. D in the parlor of Lovejoy's. *She's* the one who asked about bachelors, and that's when he started rambling about gentlemen and opportunity.

"Won't they be angry?" I ask.

Nell shrugs. "They won't be angry with us. They'll be angry—and rightly so—with Mr. Mercer."

The last of the men to leave is the ruddy, burly one who handed Jer the jerky. We're on the other side of the room, but he catches my eye and gives a shy little half wave.

"You've been here three hours and already you've got a sweetheart?" Ida teases.

"He tried to feed my brother shoe leather." I pet Jer's hair. "It was odd, but kind."

"You won't find anyone kinder than Mr. Wright," Nell says. "He's the one I feel sorry for. He came all this way, and he'll go home empty-handed. Yet again."

"Don't gossip, Nell." Julia puts down the ten of clubs.

"What? It's true." Nell scowls at her cards. "He's not the sort of man any of us will look at twice. For my part, I couldn't marry someone who already got his heart broken."

My heart got broken in moments and hours and days. First, the casualty list had to be wrong. Then, there had to be two Henry Demings in the regiment, both from Windward, and the dead one was not my father. At length the parcel came from Papa's commanding officer with his watch and a packet of letters from us, and that's when he was really gone.

Mrs. D got her heart broken at the same stroke and turned prickly and short with everyone, even neighbors who also knew loss. Even me. Especially me, and especially if I cried in front of her. She could bear it, she said, if she didn't have to think about it, and if I was *falling to pieces* she'd have to think about it.

Then Jer was born, and I finally had someone to talk to. Someone who didn't mind if I cried. Someone else who needed a papa when every last one was getting chewed up on some Southern battlefield.

So I made us flapjacks in animal shapes. I told stories with silly voices. I caused our broom to have an accident, then from the handle I made us a stick horse to share named Bartleby.

Getting your heart broken isn't something you can control. But you can decide whether you're going to be nasty to the neighbors or offer jerky to hungry children you don't even know, just because they're hungry.

Mrs. Grinold comes over to our table. "Jane, sweetheart, I arranged a hotel room for your family for the night. Your stepmother's there now. I promised I'd take you and Jer up and make sure you latched the door behind you."

"Yes, ma'am," I say, even though I thought Mrs. Yesler was going to take care of everything. "Is she all right?"

Mrs. Grinold smiles faintly. "When I left, she was ranting about finding Asa Mercer and giving him a piece of her mind. And about how he should be grateful she's a lady or she'd also give him a black eye. So, yes. I think she'll be all right."

At least Mrs. D isn't talking about going back to Lowell.

I tell my friends good night and carry a sleepy Jer upstairs behind Mrs. Grinold. The room has clean whitewashed walls and a big iron bedstead made up with colorful blankets. The window faces away from the town, toward the dark, dense woods that roll up the hill and out of sight. There's also a church back there, painted white like everything else in Seattle. As if people want to be exactly sure where the mud and cedar stop and the town begins.

If there's a church, there's got to be a school.

Mrs. D is in front of the mirror, busily wrapping her hair in rags to make curls. Her Sunday dress hangs on a peg by the window, sponged clean of the worst grime. She's muttering very dark things about Mr. Mercer to her narrow-eyed reflection.

I put Jer to bed, then pull the pamphlet out of my carpetbag and read just the improvements.

It's *got* to look better tomorrow. This is Washington Territory, after all. A whole continent away from everything we left behind.

The bachelors are in the parlor again first thing when Jer and I come down to breakfast. To a man, they stand up when I walk through toward the dining room. When they see it's a kid and not one of the Mercer Girls, they slump into their chairs and wring their hats and go back to studying the doorway.

All except Mr. Wright. He holds up a piece of jerky and makes a show of gnawing it.

"Not for eat!" Jer shouts.

After breakfast Jer and I visit the common in front of

the Occidental. It's situated at the tip of the triangle made by the streets. The bay and sky are the same flat gray, but at least it's not raining anymore. Some Indians are tending their canoes, and logs are bumping down the mill road and splashing into the water.

It's still early. Maybe the bustling starts up later in the day.

"C'mon, Jer," I say, "let's go find the school."

"We go inna tarij?" he asks hopefully.

"I don't know if there are even any *horses* here."

Most of the buildings are south of us, but I'm not sure which are the dens of vice Nell was talking about, so we head north.

Trees are everywhere, and they are not the spindly, spiky palms of Rio. They're leafy like oaks and bushy like fir, and they are massive. Not a one is smaller around than Jer, and lots are wider than my arm stretched out. Some lingering stumps are bigger still. They shoot up taller than anything ought to, and they smell damp and old and weather-beaten.

We come upon a house that doesn't belong on a muddy street at the edge of the world. It's two stories tall and made of milled boards with a proper brick chimney. The bay swims in reflections off real glass windows, and there's red-painted scrollwork along the porch. It's so much like our old farmhouse that I blink back sudden, hot tears.

A girl my age steps onto the porch. She's barefoot, her skirts are kilted up, and she's carrying a dented tin pail that just might hold her dinner for school.

Flora is keeping the light. Nell will spend all day being toasted at socials with Ida and Julia and the others.

It's been four months since we steamed out of New York harbor. Four months and four thousand miles, and I've been a school-boat invigilator, a naval combat veteran, a reluctant sock mill worker, a petty thief, and a whist novice. If that's not the opposite of *poor dear*, I don't know what is.

I lift a hand and call, "Hello!"

The girl waves back and comes down the walkway, swinging her pail. "You must be from the Mercer party! What a to-do, right? I'm Evie. Mother says the whole Mercer mess really is a shame, but of course that's not your fault. I never thought there'd be anyone my age. It was going to be seven hundred unmarried young ladies, and Mother couldn't say anything but *Where are we going to put them all?*"

Evie laughs, and I laugh too, because who'd have thought *no one* got what they expected from Asa Mercer?

"I'm off to meet my friends and see if the boys are

using the woods fort," Evie goes on. "You and your brother could come, if you want. If your mother says you can. Not everyone's mother is all right with her playing in the woods, but it's perfectly safe. Great fun, too."

Chances are good Mrs. D is in the parlor of the Occidental right now. She's likely sitting stiffly on a horsehide chair and making all the bachelors uncomfortable by asking each one if he knows a banker or a doctor or a lawyer who's looking for a refined East Coast wife to keep house for him.

"It's my stepmother," I reply, "and I don't think she'll mind."

Jer skips ahead of us through the puddles.

"A ship arriving is a big occasion," Evie says, "but *girls* arriving? Simply does not happen. So, believe me, my friends will be desperate to meet you. Especially if you tell us absolutely *everything* about the trip."

She links arms with me like Elizabeth used to, and all at once I'm back in the schoolyard and Jer isn't born yet and Beatrice and I are at either end of a skipping rope twirling as fast as we can while Violet's feet flash against the ground like a galloping horse.

Evie's friends are Jenny—"Eugenie, but only my mother calls me that"—and sisters Inez and Madge.

"The voyage wasn't really as tame as they say, was

it?" Madge looks skeptical and more than a little disappointed. "No storms? No pirates? No one hanged from the yardarm?"

"You'll tell us the good parts, won't you, Jane?" Inez begs. "The older girls pat us on the head and tell us to run along."

"Our very own informant." Evie nudges me as playfully as Nell might, so I do my best to answer their excited, nonstop questions, and every now and then I work in one of my own.

Are you really from Boston? Lowell? Where's that? What was it like on the ship? That Mr. Mercer, can you believe his nerve? My father says he'll skip town before too long. Town? Sure, we'll show you around! Up north of the mill road's where people live, and south of it is where the stores and such are. But only on Commercial Street and some parts of Occidental Street. The rest we call down on the sawdust because it used to be all tidelands till old Dutch Ned started dumping the sawdust from Yesler's mill to fill it in. Down on the sawdust's where all the card rooms and gambling parlors and other places we're not supposed to know about are. Come, let's start with the bakery.

The bakery is a breath of yeasty goodness against the brine, and there are several general stores, a brewery, a druggist, a photographer, a few eateries, a newspaper, and a *dress shop.*

And no looms. Not a single clattery, bothersome one.

No one's talking about handsome officers or fashionable hats. Inez is hoping we can play dolls later—*we*—and Jenny's pointing out the best berry bushes, and Evie swings her pail like we're listening for the school bell.

I love Flora and Nell dearly, but both thought hopscotch was a baby game.

"Where's the school?" I ask.

Evie sighs, but Inez helpfully points up the hill at a stately white building perched on a knoll. "That's our university. We haven't even been a territory fifteen years, and already we've got a proper university."

"Just because your uncle donated the land . . . ," Jenny mutters.

"That's not the mayor's house?" I peer at it again.

Evie snickers. "We haven't even got a mayor."

"But . . . what about school for kids?" I ask. "You all go to school. Right?"

"Sure we do," Madge says. "Whenever there's a school running."

"You mean you're already out for summer?" I frown. "It's nowhere near warm enough."

Jenny's squinting like she's trying to recall. "Mrs. Carr taught a summer session a few years ago. Remember?"

"Oh, and Miss Gallagher, who came with Mr. Mercer's

first expedition, taught us last winter," Inez puts in. "I liked her. It's a shame she got married."

My mouth is going dry. "That's not right. School just . . . *is*. It gets out for the summer because it's so hot, then in autumn when the weather's cooler, you come back."

"That's the way it works back East, you mean," Jenny says. "There's nothing like that here. We go when there's a teacher willing to teach us and our parents have money to pay for it."

"Another girl who came with Mr. Mercer's first expedition keeps writing letters to the territorial legislature. Antoinette Baker. She's trying to make them give money to build a schoolhouse here in Seattle, so everyone can go and no one has to pay." Madge kicks a rock. "That sounds like what you mean."

"To pay *her* to be the teacher," Evie adds with a grin.

I've stopped walking. Right in the middle of the street. "No. No, there have to be schools."

"Maybe one of the girls who came on your boat will offer lessons," Jenny says. "Then, I imagine we'll all go. You're nearly twelve, right? Like Inez and Evie? The three of you will probably be able to sit together. I promise I won't pull your hair."

Ida would have told me. *Nell* would have told me.

Only all they can talk about is how many socials they're invited to. How Seattle can't get enough of hearing how the Mercer Girls fared on their wondrous voyage.

"Jane? Are you all right?"

Mr. Mercer's original advertisement in the *Times* said his ship would carry seven hundred girls and women. They could not all have been meant to be schoolteachers.

Three hundred dollars is a lot of money, and no one can make a girl get married. You can nudge her, though, if you promise her a job teaching in schools that aren't there.

"No," I whisper. "I'm sorry. I must go."

Miss Gower, the Old Maid of the Territory, had to go to Olympia to get a school. She wouldn't have been swayed or distracted by the Seattle ladies' socials and fawning. She must have asked around and learned the truth, so she boarded that steamer and never looked back.

Evie takes my elbow. "You all go ahead. I'll meet you at the big tree. I'm going to see Jane and her brother back to their hotel. She looks *greensick*."

I never thought much of school until it started being more than slates and recitations. Everything I wanted school to be seemed possible in Washington Territory in a way it didn't anywhere else.

In Lowell the landlord would still want his rent. Mrs. D would still be flinging shuttles for fourteen hours a day to pay it while growing slowly more bitter with every warp and weft. My friends would still idle past the common pump complaining how dreary lessons were while I dragged Jer here and there and worried at my blisters till they burst.

We left that behind, though. The Washington Territory in Mr. Mercer's pamphlet has no landlords. It has no looms. It has neatly turned-out gentleman bachelors and a climate to rival Rio and schoolhouses on every corner.

It's all lies, though. Every word Mr. Mercer wrote or said. That means he didn't care who came on the *Continental*. We could have had any sort of mind or constitution. We were all brought here because Mr. Mercer took wheelbarrows full of money from big, angry men who swing axes and picks all day.

We are here because of what we can do for others, not for how we might improve ourselves.

The walk back is a blur of mud. Evie carries Jer, even though his dirty feet muck up her apron, and she keeps up a constant stream of chatter. *So sorry you're feeling poorly, Jane, but when you're better, you really do have to come see our woods hideout. Inez and Madge's cousins built it, but they don't use it much since they got hired to raft timber out to the sloops . . .*

By the time we get back to the Occidental, I can't see straight. I thank Evie stiffly and plow up to our room, towing Jer by the sleeve. He squawks, but I don't care. I slam the door and go right for my carpetbag. I pull out Mr. Mercer's pamphlet and heave up the window sash and *fling* that pack of lies as far into the woods as I can.

Nothing about Washington Territory is the way Mr. Mercer said it would be, and there's nothing we can do about it.

13

MRS. YESLER ALREADY HAS A GIRL STAYING WITH her. So do Mrs. Denny and Mrs. Terry and every other missus in town with a space to spare.

"We planned for single girls," Mrs. Yesler says. "We had no idea there'd be . . . children."

So Jer and Mrs. D and I stay on in the Occidental along with the other widows in the expedition, since there are no more hearths or floors available. My friends are all safely tucked away, though. There's not even one girl left to play whist or chat with after supper.

They're all up the street and around the corner. Just like Flora said. Only, they're never in, because every woman with a sawhorse table wants to feed them up on tea and cakes and hear their stories again and again. All of them together, like a regiment of combat veterans.

Mr. Condon at the registry desk tells Mrs. D the boarding bill will be six dollars a week. It sounds like a lot, but she doesn't even blink. I know she's bad at ciphering, so I cipher for her.

There's twelve invigilating dollars tucked away in the toe of Jer's old baby shoe. I first thought there'd be sixteen, but I hadn't figured on staying almost three weeks in San Francisco or finishing the journey on a lumber schooner. Still, it's twelve more dollars than we started with.

Twelve dollars means two weeks in the Occidental and an empty baby shoe. Or one week and new clothes for the fancy wedding Mrs. D will surely want.

Or three weeks and owing someone else in addition to Mr. Mercer.

"All the best ones are married already," Mrs. D complains to Mrs. Grinold at breakfast. "The others only have eyes for these empty-headed girls. Like the rest of this town. So much blither-blather about how wonderful these *Mercer Girls* are. Like those silly pieces were the only ones who made that dreadful trip."

Those *silly pieces* are my friends. It's not their fault the officers on the *Continental* took one look at Jer and me and glided their eyes right over Mrs. D in favor of girls like Ida and Nell.

"Maybe you're being too choosy." Mrs. Grinold stabs at her porridge with a bent spoon. "Besides, you didn't come on the early schooners. Some of those ladies who are fighting to get the girls in their parlors now could barely hide how annoyed they were with more mouths to feed."

"I've still got irons in the fire," Mrs. D says with a smile she must imagine to be mysterious. "I'm not going to rush to the altar with just anyone."

"Have you talked with Mr. Wright at all?" I ask. "Because he's really quite clever if—"

"No, Jane." Mrs. D sighs big. "Honestly. Now, Marjorie, I wonder if you've . . ."

I help Jer pour molasses on his flapjacks. She's just not giving the bachelors in the parlor a chance. There has to be at least one who'd make a good husband.

I was only six when Papa and Mrs. D were married. At supper one night Papa told me I'd be getting a new mother—steps were for walking down. My mother died from a fever when I was quite small, and having a mother again sounded nice. There'd be cookie-baking and quilt-piecing, just like my friends and their mothers. I could wear hair ribbons again because mothers knew how to tie proper bows.

The girl who became Mrs. D appeared one day in our

pew at church. Before the service Papa introduced her as Miss Chandler. I smiled politely like I'd been taught and asked, "Are you coming to school with me tomorrow? The big girls are very nice. I'm sure they'll take to you right away."

Papa laughed aloud.

The future Mrs. D smiled quick and stabby. "I've no need of school. I'm marrying your father."

During church that day I ignored Miss Chandler gazing adoringly at Papa and studied the unmarried girls and women. If I'd known Papa planned to choose my new mother so soon, I'd definitely have had some suggestions.

So I'd be a *silly piece* myself if I didn't try to work out which of the bachelors in the Occidental's parlor would best fit the bill. The fact that they're still turning up every day—hat in hand, combed and hopeful—definitely helps their cause. At least half a dozen disappointed bachelors have already departed for their mines or homesteads or logging camps, leaving behind strings of threats against one Asa Mercer.

I don't want anyone with violence on his mind. You can't live through a war and its poverty-making and its haunted veterans and come out believing any fist-and-knuckle, gun-and-cannon solution will ever solve a thing.

Even for someone like Mr. Mercer and his brazen lies. Even for Nell's scoundrel of a brother.

When I go into the parlor, the bachelors stand up. They know I'm too young for courting, but they also know I'm friendly with the girls who aren't. By my third day in the hotel each of them had introduced himself most courteously with the hope I'd say nice things about the encounter to my friends.

Mr. Singer isn't here today. He must have finally given up on Julia. Mr. Davis wants to know if Nell is going to the big meeting later at Yesler's Hall.

"What meeting?"

"Asa Mercer's going to give an account of himself," Mr. FitzHugh replies darkly. "He owes me three hundred dollars, and he owes this town an explanation."

He owes me an explanation too. Me and Mrs. D and every one of my friends who came here thinking he was an honest broker.

Mr. W is whittling what looks to be Hoss's little wooden friend. There's curly shavings all over his big belly and a few caught in his beard.

"My brother has a toy like that," I say.

"Then I imagine he'd fancy another." Mr. W smiles. "I'll make you one too if you like. What animal?"

I open my mouth to say *I'm too old for toys*. But I miss

my dolls. I miss my skipping rope. I miss the little tin tea set my grandmother gave me when I turned five.

"How about a fish?"

"You shall have it."

None of these bachelors are bankers, but if there's no banker within a week's paddle, Mrs. D could at least look up from her moaning and *talk* to men like Mr. W. She could be missing out on something just as good, but in a different way.

As he whittles, Mr. W tells me about his time in the Fraser River valley during the gold rush. Pretty soon I'm giggling at his stories of harried camp cooks and miners chased by bears and a furious one-eyed lady prospector who swore as much as three deckhands put together.

By dinner two more bachelors have left the parlor. They want to get good seats at the front of the hall so Mr. Mercer will hear every bad word they plan to shout at him. Mrs. D comes in with Jer, and Mr. W offers to walk us down to the meeting.

"Sure!" I say, before Mrs. D can politely refuse.

She fixes a smile and drops Jer into my arms. It's not far from the hotel to Yesler's Hall, but Jer and I get there way before Mrs. D and Mr. W. Even I can tell Mr. W's dragging his feet and taking his sweet time.

I like Mr. W, but he's no banker or storekeeper. He's

not handsome. Not even if you squint. He's got a plain, round face, and he walks like a deckhand. He doesn't stand a chance against Mrs. D's picture of the sort of man she's decided Seattle owes her.

Yesler's Hall is packed. The moment Mr. Mercer appears on a platform at the front, people shout questions at him. Also accusations. And plain old swears. Reverend Bagley holds up his hands and launches into a boring speech about the rightness of Mr. Mercer's enterprise and how he did a service to Seattle and should be thanked instead of taken to task.

It's hot and close in here. Jer's getting restless. Not even Hoss will keep him busy for long. I can't leave, though. I won't get another chance like this.

Mr. Bagley is going on and on like every preacher ever, so I decide to sit outside on the step till he's done. Mr. Mercer certainly won't leave till he's had a chance to say his piece. The crowd won't *let* him leave till it's satisfied.

I duck under elbows. I squeeze past skirts. I tow Jer behind me inch by inch.

I'm almost at the door when Reverend Bagley starts talking about vice and moral degeneration and how good it is for the town to have more marriageable white women so there won't be any more mixing of the races.

At least a dozen people turn in my direction.

Only, they're not looking at me. They're looking at Mr. W. They must be, because he's turning shiny red, and his brows come together, and he walks out of the hall with his chin up and his gaze blank, like a soldier on parade.

Reverend Bagley goes on *something something civic pride* and the crowd turns back to Mr. Mercer, who is still standing hand-on-heart downcast like he's the one who's been wronged. Jer and I finally make it outside, where it's ten times cooler and fifty times less awkward.

Mr. W is nowhere in sight. Nell said he'd gotten his heart broken. Maybe he was married to an Indian girl, and some people in town thought it was a bad idea. Something must have happened to her, then, or Mr. W wouldn't be in the parlor of the Occidental trying to get a wife.

"I pay dere?" Jer points across the street at the Occidental's common.

"Sure, Jer, off you go."

I sit down on the step and watch Jer trot through the muddy road and pick up rocks to throw at stumps.

There are Indians everywhere in town. They paddle around in their canoes and sell things like fish and berries and work in the mill and sometimes go to church. There was nothing in the pamphlet about Indians, but I'm not too surprised about that. It would probably have been lies anyway.

Behind me the hall gets quiet, and I hear Mr. Mercer's voice. Men shout questions at him, but someone shushes them, and Mr. Mercer's allowed to give a speech that's almost as tiresome as Reverend Bagley's.

Only Mr. Mercer's boring speech is about how wrong the newspapers are to spread such slander about him. Instead of being celebrated as a hero like the last time he arrived in the company of marriageable maidens, he's unjustly accused of the worst vile villainies, and he is deeply offended that people in this town would believe such hatefulness.

All I can do is laugh.

This whole expedition was Mr. Mercer's pride and joy, and not even *he* got what he expected at the end.

The meeting lasts ages, and after a while I stop listening. All the questions sound the same, and Mr. Mercer's answers never change. Finally, people start coming out, and I stand up so I don't get stepped on. Jer is still happy playing on the common, so it's time to do what I came here for.

I put myself in front of Mr. Mercer, but he dodges around me like I'm a stump.

"Excuse me," I call. "Sir?"

"What?" He rounds on me, hostile, till he realizes I'm a child and people are watching. Then he says in a kinder voice, "Yes, my girl?"

I'm not fooled, but as I look up at Mr. Mercer—and up—I wish Nell were here so some of her brass would rub off on me.

That's when I realize I don't want an explanation. I want him to beg my pardon, and all I'm going to get is a chuck to the cheek and a *dear child*. Washington Territory is not paradise. It's just a place, and not a particularly nice one at that.

But he's standing there with a bland, treacly look on his sunburned face, so I have to say something, and what I manage is, "Um . . . when is the special market going to be?"

"Market?"

"For socks," I blather, "like you said on the ship. We all made things to sell. Like you wanted. My stepmother and I knitted socks and we really need the money and—"

"Socks?" Mr. Mercer barks it like a sergeant major. "Do you really think I have *time* to think about such *petty*—"

Then he coughs into his hand and smiles over my head at the crowd and chucks my cheek. "My dear child, please be assured it will be attended to with the utmost care."

He glides past me through the crowd to Reverend Bagley's side and away.

The utmost care.

In other words, there won't be a market and it's a darn good thing Miss Gower needed an invigilator.

In other words, I'm on my own.

14

WE'RE HEADING INTO THE DINING ROOM FOR breakfast when Mr. Condon calls Mrs. D over to the registry desk and asks if she plans to stay another week.

"Yes, I think we will," Mrs. D replies with her coy smile. Mr. Condon isn't a banker, but he doesn't have a wife, and I suspect Mrs. D might be changing her mind about how *vulgar* it would be to be married to an innkeeper.

"Very good," Mr. Condon says, like he doesn't notice her trailing curls and bitten-red lips. "If you'd kindly pay the boarding bill for last week, then."

"Th-that's not how it's done in New York!" Mrs. D forgets to be flirty. She sounds scared instead. "I'm just a helpless widow. All alone in the world and far from friends and kin."

I muffle a snort into Jer's hair. Mrs. D is a lot of things, but she's not helpless.

"Ma'am, this isn't New York." Mr. Condon smiles like he's heard it all before. "A week's worth of credit is the best I can do."

"Even for one of the Mercer Girls?"

Mr. Condon doesn't reply, and Mrs. D's whole face goes dark, because she's not one of the Mercer Girls and they both know it. She might have come on the same expedition and shared a ship with them, but that's where it ends. A widow can't be a girl, even when in a way she is, and definitely not when she's got me and Jer behind her.

"Fine." Mrs. D storms toward the stairs. "I'll be back directly."

While we wait, Jer gallops Hoss around the room and I peek into the parlor. There are no bachelors. Not a one. Not even Mr. W.

I shouldn't care, but I do. Mr. W was going to finish telling me how he found gold the first time, how he was sure it couldn't be real. Sometimes I forget he's a grown-up, since he talks to me friendly and companionable. Like Nell does, and Flora used to.

Mrs. D bustles up to the registry desk. She carefully lays out three of the two-dollar bills, counting under her

breath *one-two*, *three-four*, *five-six* like she practiced it all
the way down.

Then she beams proudly, and considering how rarely
she smiles that big—and that genuine—I smile too. It
must be hard when you can't cipher properly. You have
to trust that people aren't cheating you. It's not like you
can catch them in the act.

Longhand division is worth something after all.

Mr. Condon picks up the bills. "Ma'am . . . this is only
three dollars' worth of currency."

"No. I—I did it right." Mrs. D blinks rapidly as her
cheeks go shiny pink. "I counted six."

"Those are two-dollar bills," I say to Mr. Condon.
"She did count it right. It's six dollars."

Mrs. D straightens and lifts her chin, just like I did
when Miss Gower asked what I thought of something.

"Yes," Mr. Condon replies patiently, "that's what
it says on the money, but the war depreciated all these
greenbacks till they're barely worth the paper they're
printed on. I'm being *generous* when I'm giving you fifty
cents on the dollar."

"Out here you folks barely even knew there was a
war!" I protest, and even as Mr. Condon is snorting a
laugh, I wish I'd set *fire* to that stupid pamphlet or turned
it into a privy rag.

Mrs. D turns her back to Mr. Condon and fans out the rest of my invigilating money like it's printed in some foreign language.

"You should give him the rest of the bills," I tell her quietly. "That will make seven-eight, nine-ten, eleven-twelve. That's six pairs of numbers altogether, which makes six dollars."

Mrs. D swallows hard. She looks mad as a wet cat, but defeated, too, and Mrs. D never looks defeated.

At last she scrubs her eyes and throws her shoulders back. She's Mrs. D again when she turns to Mr. Condon and smacks the money on the counter much harder than she needs to.

"I believe that settles up for last week." Her voice is prim and cold. "Now I must feed my children."

Mrs. D turns on her heel and marches toward the dining room, all rustling skirts and bobbing hat-plumes. I collect Jer and promise him breakfast, wondering with every step if I heard her right.

Jer eats a huge stack of flapjacks that he coats with at least a gallon of molasses. Since there are no bachelors to watch her eat, Mrs. D orders a big plate of eggs and hash and puts it away like a deckhand.

I can barely swallow my bread and jam.

One week from today Mr. Condon's going to need

another six dollars from us. Since Mrs. D's grand plan to marry a banker has gone the way of the pamphlet, that means one of us has to find employment.

No looms in Seattle. Not a single familiar, lucrative one.

Mrs. D came to Washington Territory so she could keep house and let someone else go out to work. I reckon that someone will have to be me.

After breakfast I go to the Carr house and ask Nell if she knows of anyone planning to open a school.

Nell's fluttering around the looking glass hanging from a nail in the kitchen. "You sound angry. You're not still angry, are you? Because I told you—I didn't *know* there weren't any schools. I'm no schoolma'am, Janie. You can't have spent four months in my company and ended up with that notion anywhere in your head."

"I'm not angry," I reply, and I try to sound like I mean it. "It's just . . . invigilating for Miss Gower was a job I could do, and it would be even better to help one of our friends with her class."

"Hmm." Nell bites her lips red, then makes a kissy-face at the mirror. "No. I haven't heard a word. We've only just arrived, though, and we're all so busy! Yet another tea this morning, then a wagon ride up to see Lake Union and a picnic there. Can you make my bow pretty?"

She wiggles her rump at me, and I fluff and straighten the loops of puffy cloth even though they'll probably get crushed in the wagon. When I'm done, Nell hugs me fierce and says, "If I hear anything, you'll be the first to know. Promise."

Back in San Francisco, Flora said there was plenty of work to go around in Seattle. I just have to figure out where.

In the Occidental's parlor, I find a newspaper that fell between two chairs. It's called *Puget Sound Weekly*, and I skim it eagerly for a Situations Available section. There are only four tiny pages that seem to be gossip and advertisements and news from *the States*, which is what they call the actual United States in this place that's still a territory.

If two girls can tend a lighthouse on some wind-blasted island, there has to be a million things they can do in Seattle. I follow the advertisements one by one, all down Commercial Street and up Occidental and as far along the mill road as Mr. Yesler's flatiron building.

The bakery won't hire me, not even to sweep up. There are a lot of dry goods and clothing and general stores, but none want counter help. Mr. Cheong at the cigar shop has jobs for boys but not girls. He's the kindest to me of all the shopkeepers, and I'm glad I saw plenty of Chinese people in San Francisco, so I don't stare.

The newspaperman who runs the *Puget Sound Weekly* doesn't need a reporter or someone to help work the press, but he does give me a sheaf of blank ragpaper dotted with spilled ink, which he planned to use as blotting paper.

I don't bother asking at the tannery or the foundry, and I don't dare go farther down on the sawdust, because I'm fairly sure whist isn't one of the card games being gambled on there. My secret hope is the millinery, but neither Mrs. Libby nor Mrs. Shorey needs a girl right now. Not that I know a thing about dressmaking. Only I didn't know how to change diapers once either.

I wish I'd kept Mr. Mercer's stupid pamphlet long enough to cross out the Industry chapter heading and scratch a correction in the margin: *Nothing but timber and more timber and STILL YET MORE TIMBER. Which is fine enough if you are a boy or a man. Otherwise, Mr. Yesler will not hire you to work at the mill. He will laugh somewhat unkindly if you ask.*

Pinkham's General Store is a stone's throw from the Occidental. After watching Mr. Pinkham going all goosey around Ida, I bring in every pair of socks Mrs. D and I knitted and pile them on the counter. I don't even have to remind him how Ida and I might as well be sisters. Mr.

Pinkham knows me on sight, and he buys the lot for three dollars to resell and doesn't blink or protest when I insist on coins instead of bills.

Three is half of six. I'm halfway there.

I should have gotten the deckhands to teach me poker.

If only Miss Gower hadn't left. If there'd have been a school in Seattle, she might have stayed. I might be invigilating for her right now.

At this rate we'll owe so much no one will marry Mrs. D even if she's the prettiest woman in the territory. All the pretty in the world won't be worth the debts she'll come with.

I trudge up to our hotel room, muddy to the knees, and glare out the window where I threw Mr. Mercer's pamphlet. There's no sign of it. Good riddance.

If Mr. Mercer's pamphlet is wronger than wrong, I'll have to make my own.

I fold the sheets of paper I got from the newspaperman in half and then quarters. The Occidental's cook gives me a piece of string and I stitch up the spines. Then I slit the folded parts to make pages. It's a book now. Just like the one Miss Bradley gave me. Only I made it myself.

In big letters across the cover I write *REFLECTIONS UPON WHAT'S NOT GOING*. There's probably some way in Latin to make it clever, but Miss Gower isn't here to help me anymore.

Then I whisper *good luck*, just in case that's part of what holds little books like this one together.

15

WHEN IT'S TIME TO PAY THE BOARDING BILL, I make Jer come with me—he'd rather be playing carriage with Jimmie Lincoln—and do my darnedest to make Mr. Condon feel guilty as sin if he even considers putting us out. Mr. Condon sighs like he's got a bellyache, but he takes my three dollars as a deposit. We can stay another week on credit, but the whole bill must be paid in full when due or the law will get involved.

Nell thinks she can get me invited on the boat trip she's going on. Madge and Inez want me to come to their cousins' woods fort with them and Evie and Jenny.

That all sounds like good fun, but I'd better start knitting. Lowell's not as far away as any of us thought.

The sun is actually trying to shine, so I collect my

half-made sock and tell Jer we're going to the common. As we pass the parlor, I catch a sliver of red flannel and—a frock coat? I skid to a stop and Jer bumps into me. There is indeed a bachelor in the parlor, and it's Mr. W! He's wearing a shabby suit that's clearly borrowed and grinning like he just struck it rich.

"You're back!" I squeal. "I thought you'd gone with the others. I'm glad you didn't, because I want to hear what happened . . . when . . ."

I trail off when I notice Mrs. D sitting next to him like she's taking tea with the president; uncomfortable but not entirely unhappy.

"Oh. Ma'am. It's just he's been telling me ab—"

"I'm marrying Mr. Wright," Mrs. D cuts in, and she says it ordinary, like she's describing the color of the parlor walls. "We're going to see the preacher at noon, then we'll be leaving the hotel for our new home."

My mouth falls open.

"What do you think, Jane?" Mr. W leans forward, forearms on his knees, looking like he really does want to know what I think, even if he's not using big words to get it out of me.

"I . . . reckon," I finally manage. "I mean, I'm not the one marrying you."

Mrs. D grunts a little pained sigh, but Mr. W smiles.

"In a way, you are. We're going to be a family, all of us together. Your stepmother is becoming my wife, sure, but that makes you and Jer my children. That's how it works."

We're all Demings now.

Only now I suppose we'll be all Wrights.

"Some men just get a wife when they marry," Mr. W adds, "but I'm lucky enough to get a family ready-made for me. I'll admit I don't know a lot about girls, though. No sisters. Um . . ."

He holds out his big hands and trails off, so what he probably means is that he's looking forward to having a son to help him with his work. Jer's real sweet, and they've already formed a bond over inedible jerky.

"I've packed the trunk." Mrs. D nods toward the staircase. "You'll want to go wash up before the wedding. I'll sort Jer out. Make sure you have everything. We won't be coming back here."

I nod and hurry upstairs to our room. I even dip the washrag in the bowl of water she left on the dressing table and scrub my neck. Then I get my carpetbag out from under the bed, stuff my knitting inside, and check to be sure everything's still there.

It feels too light without Mr. Mercer's pamphlet. Even if that thing was nothing but lies. I look out the window where I flung it, but of course it's nowhere in sight. It's probably fallen apart in the rain by now, or sunk deep in the mud. Which is a fitting fate, considering how the rotten thing mentioned neither rain nor mud.

When I go back downstairs, Mr. W is handing silver dollars to Mr. Condon. Mr. Condon slides a paper across the registry desk, and the two shake hands.

Now I understand. Mr. W is paying the rest of our boarding bill. The three dollars left from last week and this week's six dollars on top of that. Mrs. D has no other way to pay it—she can't teach school, there are no looms—so she has to marry someone who'll take her and Jer and me. Who has enough money to pay off all the flapjacks and molasses and biscuits and bacon we stuffed ourselves with.

Mrs. D came four thousand miles to get married. She had it all planned out, and her plan involved a banker and a pretty new dress and a fancy church and the whole town turned out for the shivaree.

There is no pretty dress. Mr. W is not a banker. I don't know what he is. I don't know where he lives or what he likes to eat or if he goes to church or chapel or meeting like Mama did once upon a time.

I don't know much about him at all. The one thing I do know is that Mrs. D could have chosen a whole lot worse.

Mrs. D is waiting nearby. She meets my eyes, then looks down. Mrs. D never looks down.

"All clean?" she asks briskly.

"Yes, ma'am." I peer into her face. "Are you crying?"

"No. Hush."

"I thought to bring the trunk down, but I couldn't manage it myself. I'm sorry."

Mrs. D. swallows and lifts her chin. "Don't worry. The baggage will be waiting when we get back from the church."

"Ma'am?"

"What, Jane?"

"Congratulations," I say softly.

That's when she hugs me. It's not a proper hug, not like she gives Jer, but she puts a quick arm over my shoulder and pulls me against her, hard and sure and fierce.

Mrs. Yesler rallies some of her neighbors, so there are a dozen people including us in the white church behind the Occidental Hotel.

Mrs. Grinold and Mrs. Horton are both there, but none of my friends from the *Continental* turn up. Not even Julia Hood, who's boarding with the Yeslers. Mrs. Yesler spills over, apologizing for Julia. She explains there's a social for the girls going on in the old Blaine orchard, and Julia really didn't think anyone would miss them.

That's where Nell must be. Nell, who was fortunate enough to fall in with friends when she found herself high and dry.

Mr. Mercer is absent as well. Considering we still owe him, I thought for sure he'd be blocking the altar until money changed hands.

My Seattle friends turn up together. Evie brings some wildflowers that are odd but pretty, and Madge and Inez picked proper flowers from their mother's impressive garden, so we all have bouquets. Jer holds my hand and whacks me across the knees with a tall iris Jenny gave him.

Just as Reverend Bagley is starting the vows, Nell rushes into the church and plows right to the front.

"I'm not too late, am I?" Nell throws her arms around me, then whispers into my neck, "The social is nice and all, but I couldn't leave you here by yourself. Not for this."

Evie and the others stare like Queen Victoria just arrived in their midst. I hug Nell back and make room for her at my elbow. I tug apart my bouquet and give her half.

Once we're settled, Reverend Bagley finishes the

vows. Mr. W and Mrs. D are pronounced man and wife. One in the sight of God.

Jer swings his iris cheerfully, his little suit already tight across his chest. He won't remember this wedding. He won't recall the exact moment his family stopped being his family and became this *other* family that includes some strange new person.

More's the point, he'll always belong to this new family in a way I never will. He's Mrs. D's flesh and blood. I'm left over from a family that doesn't exist anymore, that got pulled apart like hot biscuits the moment Mama felt that first sniffle come on.

Nell lingers as departing guests wish the new couple well, but soon she says she ought to get back to the social. "I'll stay if you really want me to, Jane, but Mrs. Dalton saw me leave, and I'd feel terrible if she took it personally. She went to so much trouble."

"That's all right," I reply, even though I wish my *Continental* friends were slightly less beloved by the town.

Nell says farewell to each of my Seattle friends one by one. They all stand straighter, like they're reciting something important.

My Seattle friends don't leave with the other guests. Inez and Madge stay so long they have to be collected by their father, and Evie and Jenny linger till Mrs.

Bagley shoos them out so she can tidy the church.

Just two weeks ago our schooner rounded the point and a sprinkling of white buildings came into view, and Seattle was beautiful and perfect for the very last time.

"Well then!" Mr. W slaps his belly with both hands. "The first thing to do is lay in some supplies before we head home."

Mrs. D heads right to the counter of Pinkham's General Store and sets the shop boy scrambling for cornmeal and flour, but Mr. W pauses outside where an Indian woman is sitting on a blanket next to some things she's made out of . . . tree bark, I think. Or long grasses. She has hats and baskets and shoes with braided ties instead of buttons or buckles. I hold Jer's hand when he tries to touch a bumpy-looking mat tight-woven in dark and pale stripes.

"*Ik-tah kunsih?*" Mr. W kneels and points to a tidy pile of bright blankets, the kind that were on the beds at the Occidental Hotel.

I can't have heard right.

The woman frowns like she's considering. "*Kalltan.*"

Or maybe Mr. W really is speaking Indian.

Mr. W reaches into his pocket and pulls out a handful of bullets. She helps herself to half, then hands him the top two blankets off the pile.

"*Mahsie, klootchman,*" he says politely, and she nods to him just as nice.

"I'll be!" I glance in wonder between the woman and Mr. W. "Did your wife teach you to speak Indian? I mean, before she died? I mean . . ."

Mr. W flinches like I slapped him. "My *what?*"

I bite my lip. "I'm sorry. That was rude, wasn't it? You're probably still sad about it."

He doesn't seem sad, though. Just bewildered.

"I've never been married at all," Mr. W replies, slow, like maybe he missed something and doesn't want to look foolish. "Not until about twenty minutes ago."

"Oh. Golly." My cheeks are getting warm. "I suppose . . . I heard you got your heart broken. Then at the meeting with Mr. Mercer . . ."

"Ahhhh." Mr. W nods big. "I see. All right. She had—has—other names, but I knew her as Louisa. I loved her something fierce. She's an Indian. A Suquamish Indian. She lives on the Port Madison reservation now. I courted her. I wanted to spend the rest of my life with her. I'm certainly not ashamed of her, like some people in this town think I should be. She's the one who's ashamed of me, and rightly."

I frown. "Why didn't you marry her? You loved her. Didn't she love you?"

Mr. W smiles sadly. "She did. Only I . . . made some mistakes. I didn't understand exactly how badly I'd fouled things up. I tried to make it right, but it was too late. One day Louisa told me to go away and not come back. So I went."

"But why didn't you fight to win her back? Why didn't you make her change her mind?"

"I'm not in the business of making folks do things." Mr. W shrugs. "She didn't want to be with me. That hurt, but making her come with me wouldn't have made either of us happy."

Jer tugs on my hand, and even though he's not the same as a sweetheart, it's hard to think what I'd do if he never wanted to see me again.

Mr. W doesn't go on, and then it's too quiet, too solemn for a wedding day, so I ask, "If your sweetheart didn't teach you to speak Indian, how did you learn?"

"It's not Indian. Not Lushootseed, that is. It's Chinook. Everyone knows it around here. You have to. Don't worry, you'll learn soon enough."

"Chinook?"

"It's a mix-up of French, English, and several different Indian languages," Mr. W says. "Chinook sort of . . . happened after the Hudson's Bay Company started trading in the territory back when it was still part of Oregon."

I frown. "Indians speak different languages?"

"You've studied geography, haven't you? You know where Europe is, that it's made up of lots of different countries. Do all the people there speak European?"

"Of course not." I loved the big, colorful map Miss Bradley would have two of us hold up and the long pointer she'd use when we'd name the countries. "They speak French and Spanish and Italian and . . . oh."

"Just so with Indians," Mr. W says. "Sometimes the languages are alike. Sometimes they're not. The nice thing about Chinook is that everyone knows some of it, so we can get what we need from one another. Come, let's go help Mrs. Wright with the supplies."

He grins big and silly when he says *Mrs. Wright*. It makes me smile too, even if I can't think of her as anything but Mrs. D.

Mr. Pinkham's shop boy has piled all our goods on a contraption that looks like the sled I had at the farmhouse. This sled has long poles that stretch from the slats straight out, like they're meant for a horse or a donkey to get harnessed there.

Only there's no horse or donkey nearby.

Mr. W stations himself between the poles like *he's* the donkey. Maybe he's showing off for Mrs. D, since it's silly to cart our goods this way or any way when we could easily have the shop boy deliver them.

"Where's your house?" I put a hand to my eyes and peer north, where Evie said everyone lives.

"You're going to want to put your boots on, Jane," Mr. W says. "We've got a bit of a walk in front of us."

16

WE HEAD UP THE MILL ROAD THAT LEADS AWAY from Mr. Yesler's wharf straight up the hill. The houses thin out on my left, the stores disappear on my right, and nothing's ahead but a whole lot of cedar.

The trees are taller than anything I could have imagined from Mr. Mercer's pamphlet that mentions them only as lumber, tidy and milled and piled on a wharf to sell. It's hard to see how these trees could ever be reduced to lumber. Not when they're so big around you couldn't hug them with your fingers touching. Not when they're living and towering and hiding any number of bears or wolves or cougars or who *knows* what else.

Calling the mill road a *road* once we're fifty steps beyond the Occidental is a lie. As the sawdust fades, it turns into a sloppy river of mud with log skids wedged across it every ten feet or so.

Mrs. D will put a stop to this. Any moment now she'll kick up a huge, ever-loving fuss. *Screech screech I won't tolerate this walking ugh my hem is a mess we will go back to town this instant and get a decent house made of milled boards.*

She doesn't, though. She shoulders her carpetbag and walks in front of Mr. W, who's straining to pull the sled heaped with our trunk and all the things we bought from Mr. Pinkham. I bring up the rear, making sure Jer is in sight somewhere ahead of me. He's having a merry time striding through the tall grass and picking wildflowers and flinging them at me by the handful.

Toward the top of the hill the skids fade out, and what's left is a path that's been made just by people walking in the same place again and again. The ground underfoot is worn down to packed dirt, and the weeds grow up tall on either side.

The trees close in. Thick and tall and endless. Pretty soon even the sound of Mr. Yesler's mill fades away.

"Sir?" I venture. "Where are we *going?*"

"Home," Mr. W says. "Also . . . perhaps you could call me something other than *sir.*"

One of the first things Mrs. D said to me after she and

Papa got married was that under no circumstances should I ever call her *Mother* or *Mama* or anything like that. She said it made her feel positively ancient, and besides, she wasn't my proper mother. She never did say what I *should* call her, so I say *ma'am* because calling her Mrs. *Deming* makes me feel like a mill girl or a parlormaid. Like she's my employer somehow and not a relation who's supposed to take care of me.

"Like what?" I ask him.

Mr. W pulls a rag from his pocket and mops his big, sweaty forehead. "I can't expect *Father*. How about Uncle Charlie?"

"All right," I say, because I plan to avoid calling him anything at all. Not that I don't like him. I do, the way you like a pretty sunset or a cool drink of lemonade. When I woke up this morning, he was a friendly bachelor who told funny stories and kept jerky in his pockets.

Now we'll all be living in his house.

It's afternoon when we emerge onto a flat beach made of small rocks that slopes down to a shimmering stretch of water. Across the water is yet another wall of timber stretching north and south and endless. There's a canoe pulled up on the beach, wide in the middle and pointed at both ends like the ones Indians use. Mr. W pulls the sled over the rocks toward it.

This is not *a bit of a walk*.

"All righty, ladies and Jer," Mr. W says cheerfully. "Let's load up the canoe. We'll be home before you know it."

There's no sound here but the *lap-lap* of water and the *shuff-rustle* of wind in the trees and Jer's whooping as he rushes down to the waterline and scares a flock of gulls. The water and the rock-beach and the stillness are not in any way pretty—*striking* is a better word. It's the sort of thing that ought to be in Mr. Mercer's pamphlet. A chapter on Sportsman's Paradise or Majestic Scenery, maybe, and it wouldn't need improvement or correction.

But over my shoulder is the trodden path that leads back to Seattle and its half-dozen roads and stores and hotels and Indian women selling things made from woven wood and everyone speaking a made-up language that belongs to everyone and no one all at once.

All my friends, too. My *Continental* friends and my Seattle friends. All of us together.

"Ready, Jane?" Mr. W stands next to the canoe. Mrs. D is already sitting in the middle, holding Jer on her lap. Our things are piled around her, some before and some behind. He's even dismantled the sled and packed it along the sides. There's a space at the front where Mr. W is pointing. "Off we go!"

Mr. W whistles as he paddles. The canoe looks like it would be shaky, but it glides steadily as we move across the lake. The sky is a pale gray, as un-Mediterranean as a thing can be, and the wind is bitter and cutting even though it's blasted *June*.

"What's the place called?" I ask Mr. W. "Where you live?"

"Where *we* live," Mr. W says in that irritatingly cheerful voice. "It doesn't have a name. Hardly anyone lives there. Seattle folk call it *the Eastside*, because it's on the east side of the lake."

"So . . . there's no town," I say.

"Heavens no!" Mr. W chuckles as if I suggested the president would be there.

Now Mrs. D will get angry. *Screech screech four thousand miles unacceptable how dare you drag me into the wilderness.*

She's not even scowling, though. All right, she *is* scowling, but that's because Jer won't stop fussing for a bite to eat or a turn at paddling or Hoss.

That means she knew. She knew marrying Mr. W meant we wouldn't be staying where there were roads and stores and friends.

We paddle past the tree-spiky piece of land to starboard. Mr. W says it's an island where Indians fish and not the Eastside where we're going. I peer for a wharf or a dock or a gravel beach, but there's none to be seen. Just cedars and water and the odd bird winging overhead. We get closer to the shore, and the trees are so tall they feel fragile, like the smallest gust could knock them down.

"Here we are!" Mr. W glides the canoe up to a platform of wide stumps that stick out of the water about the length of my forearm. They're clustered so tightly they form something of a landing. He climbs out of the canoe and strings a length of rope across the stump dock and well into the trees beyond.

"All secured," Mr. W says when he returns. "Let me carry Jer up to dry land."

While Mrs. D hands Jer over, I crawl out of the canoe. It bumps and wavers against the dock, and the water below looks bleak and cold. The stumps are mushy underfoot, and all at once I wonder how far down they go. If they're sturdy enough to trust.

"Too high! No up! Daney! Daney!"

I hurry across the landing and scrabble up the slippery, cedary bank. Jer has been sat on a stump that's as high as my waist. He's stiff with terror and red from squalling.

"Come now, Jer, you're all right." I help him off the stump.

"If you let him down, watch him, got that?" Mr. W

says over his shoulder. "The shoreline here is treacherous. There are places where you can fall straight through,
places that look like they'd be all right to stand on. I put
him up there so we could unload without worrying about
him getting trapped under some roots."

And drowning, he means, but thankfully doesn't say.

I turn to Jer and tell him, "You don't have to be on
the stump if you sit right here next to it and *don't move*.
Play with Hoss while we get things out of the canoe. If you
move, I'll put you up there again. Savvy?"

"No up," Jer repeats, shaking his head firmly. "Daney,
hold you."

"I can't hold you, Jer," I reply. "I've got to help unload.
You need to sit down now."

"*Hold you, Daney!*" Jer shrieks, loud enough to bring
Mr. W clumping over and fumbling in his pockets and
looking annoyed.

I make a fist like Nell showed me and stay between
him and Jer.

Mr. W kneels and pulls out a little wooden animal and
holds it up without a word. Jer stops howling and peers
first at the toy, then at Mr. W.

"It's a bear," Mr. W says to him. "It's for you, but only
if you sit here and play with it while your sister helps with
the load."

The bear isn't as cleverly carved as Hoss, but I grin outright at its round, furry rump and slightly crossed eyes. I thought Mr. W had forgotten all about those toys he was making for us.

Jer takes the bear and plunks down beside the stump. He neighs and beams and holds it up. "Hoss, Daney. Other Hoss."

"If you say so," I reply, because it doesn't do any good to argue with a little kid. Or maybe Jer thinks every wooden toy is a horse. Maybe he'll think my fish is a horse too.

"Charles, I need your help with this!" Mrs. D is struggling with a sack of meal, so Mr. W hauls it up for her. He makes trip after trip, puffing and wheezing to get the heaviest things up the bank and onto dry ground.

His pockets look empty.

I'll ask. I'll just come out and say it, like Miss Gower would.

But it'll be awful if there's no fish. Maybe Mr. W didn't have time. Or he decided I didn't need one. Or he just forgot. He'll mutter something and turn red and I'll be the one who'll look the fool with my hand out for some baby toy I don't even need.

"Jane, you're in the way!" Mrs. D snaps. "Stop your woolgathering and help with these bags!"

So I do. I carry bag after bag and pile them on the bank while Jer gallops Other Hoss around and makes a saddle for him out of leaves. By the time we're done, I can't think how to ask without sounding greedy or selfish or babyish.

We get everything unloaded from the canoe, but Mr. W's sled won't work here to carry things, because there's no road. There's nothing but timber in every direction, and a brushy undergrowth that would catch sled runners and overturn our belongings at every step.

"We'll carry what we can," Mr. W says, "and I'll come back for the rest once you're settled in the cabin."

We get most of the dry goods into carpetbags and rucksacks. Even Jer is carrying a bag of beans with one hand and his new toy in the other. Our trunk must stay, as well as the pile of blankets and a jug of molasses.

"Will these things be safe?" I ask. "No one will take them, right? *Animals* won't get to it?"

I give him a hopeful Look.

Mr. W shoulders his load. He's carrying three times what anyone else is, and his cheeks are already pink. "We didn't leave anything animals would care about. As for people, Indians don't come here much because the fishing's better other places, and the nearest white people are busy digging coal down in Coal Creek."

"So . . . we're alone here." I can't keep the disappointment out of my voice, and it's not just because my friends are clear across the lake.

"Not in the slightest!" Mr. W grins. "We've got each other."

It might be all of us together, but we are not a *we*. You can't fling strangers into close quarters and expect them to knit into a family just like that.

Just because this is our only choice doesn't make it a good one.

The cabin sits in a clearing, small and square like something out of Mr. Grimm's stories. It's made of stacked-up logs crossed at the corners with mud mashed in the cracks. There are wooden shingles on the roof and a chimney made of smooth, round rocks.

After all the mud and ramshackle white-painted shanties in Seattle, an honest-to-goodness outpost of civilization on the fringe of a brand-new territory, I didn't expect a homestead cabin out back of the beyond to be so . . . tidy.

The cabin is a single room, with a hulking black stove opposite the front door and windows at either end covered by wooden shutters. On one side of the room is a big bed and on the other is a set of bunk beds like on the *Continental*. There's also a table with a red cloth and a bench near the hearth. On the wall by the fireplace, there's a shelf with crockery containers that look like they're supposed to hold dry goods.

Not exactly a banker's mansion, but even Mrs. D can't find fault with how it's kept.

Mr. W puts down his load and builds a fire. Once the stove is busy and crackling, the whole cabin feels more comfortable. More like a home. Mrs. D takes the crockery containers off the shelf and examines them one by one. The biggest has a dusting of cornmeal at the bottom. Then flour, and finally sugar.

"Daney!" Jer tugs my skirt. "I seed a wabbit! It dere. By da path."

"Go see if you can catch it," Mr. W says. "It would make a tasty supper."

Jer furrows his brow. "I . . . can go?"

"Charles . . . ," Mrs. D says at the same time I ask, "it's safe, right?"

"Perfectly safe as long as he stays in the clearing," Mr. W says. "We discussed this, Rose. This isn't Lowell, Massachusetts. They must learn how to be on the Pacific coast. Both of them."

Mrs. D swallows. Then she nods.

Both of them. That means me, too.

I've read Mr. Mercer's stupid pamphlet back to front

and it's nothing but lies. I *did* know how to be on the Pacific coast, until the Pacific coast was nothing like how it was supposed to be.

Mr. W crouches so he's at Jer's eye level. "Go see if you can catch that rabbit, but stay in the clearing. Hear?"

Jer looks at us. Mrs. D fidgets with the crockery lids, but I nod and smile. So he toddles outside, looking back every few steps. He edges out farther and farther till he finds a stick he can hit things with. Then something on the ground catches his eye, and he bends down for a better look.

I wait for *Jane, go mind your brother*, but Mrs. D unpacks the tea and butter in choppy, tight motions, like she needs something to busy her hands. Mr. W touches her elbow in a very small embrace, then picks up a bucket and heads outside.

Jer is *happy* out there all alone.

I don't quite know what to do with myself. I pick up a bag of beans, but Mrs. D pulls it away.

"For heaven's sake, Jane, I'm trying to work here. Shoo!"

"You . . . don't want my help?" I ask, because it's like she started talking at me in Chinook.

"Not right this moment," she says. "Once everything is put away . . . maybe. For now . . . I don't know, go learn to be here."

"Yes, ma'am."

Like there can be anything worth learning amidst nothing but timber.

I go outside and sit against the cabin. Jer's happily jumping on and off a stump near the edge of the clearing, waving his stick around. I almost call him over and ask if he wants to play. Instead, I pull out my ragpaper book and my stub of a pencil.

It will need chapters if it's to be a proper pamphlet. Trade and Industry are right out, as are Roads and Civil Government.

The Lake, then. That's my first chapter. It's what's keeping me from my friends. It's what's keeping me from what little I had gotten to know.

The shoreline cannot be trusted, I write. *If you don't know where to step, you could drown.*

Mr. W brings the bucket full of water into the cabin, then starts toward the path we came up. When he spots me, he pauses. "There are still things to put away. Did Mrs. Wright set you another task?"

I shrug. This is Mrs. D's hearth. What she's been aiming for and planning for since that day all those months ago when the farmhouse got foreclosed on and we were turned out in the road. Now that she's got it, she wants to rule it all alone.

Mr. W squints at me. "Come, let me show you the place before I get the rest of our things."

We start at the well, and Mr. W shows me how to lift and lower the wooden cover. There's a henhouse and six surly hens wandering the clearing. Mr. W tells me each of their names and explains they'll be in a better humor in a few days, once they get over being angry at him for penning them up while he was away fetching us.

There's a half-finished stable that Mr. W says he'd like to put a goat in someday, or even a milking cow if he can think of a way to get her in his canoe. He says it with a wink, so I know he's joking about the canoe part, but since cows can't swim, we're not likely to get one anytime soon.

Behind the house, facing south, is the garden. Mr. W holds both arms out like he's giving it a hug. The dug-up ground behind the deer fence is all in greening rows, and I recognize some of the vegetable tops from the farmhouse garden. There's squash in one big patch, and some beets and lettuce. Next to it is a wooden trough full of water and a scarecrow.

"One last—but very important—thing." Mr. W points to a little wooden building beyond the clearing about a stone's throw into the forest. "The privy."

I do *not* want to venture into the woods. Not unless

I'm playing in Inez and Madge's hideout with my friends. But when he says *privy*, I suddenly have to go, even though I didn't a moment before. So I pick my way through moss and damp, loamy ground and rocks. It's facing away from the cabin, so I go around to the front and—

"There's no door!" I blurt. There's a bench, at least, with a hole cut in it standing over a hole in the floor.

I will simply have to hold it in forever.

Sturdy constitution. *Sturdy constitution.*

I hike up my skirts and pull down my drawers, but I can't bring myself to sit all the way down on the bench. Our lodgings in Lowell had a frightful privy, but at least there was no moss growing on it.

When I crunch back to the clearing, Mr. W is bright red. "It was just me here for so long. I figured the birds and deer wouldn't mind." He's trying to joke, to make this moment less completely awful. "I'll make a door. Today. First thing. Right after I get back from the landing."

Mrs. D will squawk like a wrung-neck chicken when she sees this. *This* will be the thing that will make her put her foot down and insist that Mr. W move us back to Seattle *right away*, that she cannot handle the wilderness *one moment longer*.

"Jane?" Mr. W shuffles. "Things got a little hectic back on the landing. Here. This is for you. If you still want it."

He tucks a smooth wooden thing into my hand, then hurries toward the lake path before I can even thank him.

The carved fish fits in my palm and has stiff fins and a gash of a smile. I drop it into my dress pocket for safe-keeping. Then I pull out my little book, turn to the very last page, and write a reflection upon the foregoing: *If you are promised a fish and you expect a fish and then get a fish, it's a lot more than a fish.*

17

BY EVENING, THE CABIN IS *SQUARED AWAY*, AS the deckhands on the *Continental* would say. The dry goods are all in their crocks, the room is aired, the floor is swept, the beds all made, the dishes washed near the well and left to dry on the draining board, and every last thing we brought or bought has come up from the lake and found a home somewhere in the cabin.

Jer barely makes it through supper before falling asleep on the floor near the hearth. Mrs. D tucks him into the bottom bunk, and I put Hoss and Other Hoss next to his pillow.

I perch on the bench next to the fire with my knitting. If we ever have occasion to go to Seattle, I want something to sell to Mr. Pinkham. I don't want to be without coins in my pocket ever again.

Mrs. D excuses herself and goes outside. Even though the privy has a door now, I'd bet a year's worth of sock money she comes back raging.

"I've got something of yours." Mr. W pulls a folded-over wad of paper from inside his coat. "Mr. Condon at the hotel gave it to me."

I know exactly what it is, and I don't want it. I don't even want to *look* at it, much less hold it. I want nothing more to do with Mr. Mercer's ridiculous stream of falsehoods ever again.

But Mr. W looks so hopeful, like Jer when he's brought you a mud pie he wants you to taste. Mr. Condon must have figured I lost it. I did write my name ever-so-carefully on the inside cover once upon a better time.

"I dried the pages and everything," Mr. W adds proudly.

I make myself smile and take the stupid pamphlet. "Much obliged. That was kind of you. Both of you."

The cover is mud-stained, but someone carefully wiped off the worst of it. The pages dried all stiff and ripply, but none of them are unreadable. More's the pity. I flip through it a few times till Mr. W sits back, looking happy. Then I tuck it in my carpetbag and collect my knitting again.

Mrs. D comes back from the privy without a word. She

smiles as she checks on Jer, then picks up her own knitting while Mr. W whittles.

We really are here for good.

When it starts to get dark, Mrs. D says, "Bedtime, Jane."

"Yes, ma'am." I put away my knitting and go to the trunk where all our clothes are. I rummage for my nightdress.

Then I freeze.

In the farmhouse, I had my own room. With a door. In our lodgings in Lowell, it was just Mrs. D and Jer and me, and even though Jer is a boy, he's a baby more than anything, and I never worried about changing in front of him.

I grip my nightdress with both hands.

"I'll . . ." Mr. W is trying to look anywhere but at me, and stumbling toward the door. "I'll, um, go check on the chickens."

Mrs. D sighs impatiently, and I shuck off my clothes and slip my nightdress over my head and hustle up the wooden ladder to my top bunk and get under the covers.

Having a stepfather sounded all right while he was safely contained in Mrs. D's ramblings. Now he's flesh and blood. Now we're living in his house, no matter how many times he says it's *ours*.

A weed-stuffed pallet doesn't sound like it would be comfortable, but I've been walking for miles and kneeling in a canoe and hauling dry goods on my back uphill through tangly undergrowth. No wonder Jer was out like a candle so early.

I'm half-asleep when I hear Mr. W's voice.

". . . string up a curtain. First thing tomorrow. It's not much, but it's something."

"Is she complaining already?" Mrs. D sounds weary and mildly put out.

"What? No. It's proper she have some privacy." Mr. W's voice goes teasing. "Besides, I don't want to be out *checking on the chickens* when it's December and cold enough to freeze the lake solid."

I face the wall and pull out my little book. The fading fire doesn't reach the top bunk too well, but I can see enough to start a chapter about Cabins.

There is only one door, I write. *It is not where you want it to be.*

The next morning Mrs. D makes breakfast and beams when Mr. W eats three helpings and falls over himself telling her how good the porridge is. It is pretty good porridge—there's even a stir of molasses in it—but you'd think she *invented* porridge, the way he carries on.

"Clearing a stump today," he says as he gets up from the table. "Anything you need before I go?"

Mr. W is looking at Mrs. D all sappy-faced, which I have to admit is kind of sweet. It's hard to imagine Papa looking at her that way.

She shakes her head and kisses his beardy cheek. Mr. W gets halfway to the door, then backtracks so he can pat Jer's shoulder, then mine. It's clumsy, like most things Mr. W does, but he could have just kept walking.

As I'm washing the breakfast dishes out by the well, Mrs. D builds a fire in the clearing.

Drat. That means laundry. That means heaving sopping dresses and linens out of boiling water and into rinse water. Water that's got to be hauled bucket by bucket from the well. That means twisting each garment till most of the water's wrung out. Lifting each heavy thing again to peg it to the line. Lye crumbling my skin, working its way into cuts.

Just like Lowell.

"Jane! You're woolgathering again." Mrs. D aims her stirring paddle at me. "Hurry and finish those dishes, then start filling up the washtub."

"Shouldn't I watch Jer?" I call. "Hot water? Fire? Lye?"

"All during that horrid voyage, you kept fretting that

he couldn't wander and do what he liked," Mrs. D replies. "Now he can. You should be happy."

Everything was going to be different. Mrs. D would have her hearth and her husband. Jer would have his mama. Somehow, Washington Territory would make us a family by the sheer force of its wonder.

By the end of today my hands will be red and stinging from hot water and lye, and I will have split at least one nail low enough to leave it raw and aching. My friends are a lake and a skid road away, playing whist or woods fort and forgetting all about me. There can't be a school on the Eastside, not when there's barely any people, broad-minded or otherwise.

I thought nothing could be worse than Lowell, but I was wrong. Living on the Eastside is going to be worse by tenscore, because I'll have something to compare it to. All those weeks helping Milly and Maude move through the primer into the first reader and quizzing the boys on world capitals—now I'm back to hauling this and stirring that and scrubbing that other thing, when barely a month ago I was giggling with Flora and Nell before we whispered our good-byes and pretended we would write.

The Occidental might have cost six dollars a week, but that money paid for more than bed and board.

It paid for time. It paid for someone else to carry the water and scrub the floor and change the bed linens and mind the wapatos while they're boiling.

Wapatos are like potatoes, I write in a new chapter called Food, Found and Other Wise. I try to use only words I know I can spell. *They are smaller, the size of a rabbit's paws, and you can boil or roast them. They grow where the lake is shallow, and you rake them out of the mud with—*

"Jane, honestly!" Mrs. D shakes her head, hands on hips. "There's no time for such idleness! Do you think this house runs itself? Go dump this water and fill up the bucket again."

The next time I write a reflection, I will sit in the privy.

Over porridge one morning, before Mrs. D can list all the chores for the day, Mr. W asks, "Jane, how are you with a hatchet? You think you can help me with the woodpile?"

"Charles." Mrs. D sighs like she does when someone who isn't Jer is being silly.

"The garden needs a good weeding too," he adds. "Would you rather take that on?"

It's close enough to *What do you think?* that I sit up straighter. Only there's not much of a choice between an aching back and filthy hands or aching shoulders and splintery hands.

"Honestly, Charles, you and your woodpile!" Mrs. D laughs, but when she sees he's serious, she adds impatiently, "It's a silly idea."

Of course she thinks me doing anything that isn't housework is silly. She's forgotten that keeping house isn't all stitching quilts and whipping up cake batter.

"Why?" Mr. W looks her right in the eye.

Mrs. D flaps her lips a few times but nothing comes out. I try hard not to grin.

"Because—because—because of *Jer*, that's why!" Mrs. D furiously cuts a piece of toasted bread into fingers for Jer. "Because she has *responsibilities*, and I can't be expected to—"

"We want a fire all winter, right?" Mr. W doesn't even raise his voice. "Then I need a helper. There's lots more to living out here than keeping house. Besides, you do that so expertly, you'll hardly miss Jane."

Mrs. D's whole face changes. She kind of . . . preens. Then she turns to me and says, "The dishes are still your responsibility, miss. After that, you're to help Mr. Wright with the chopping and whatnot. The *moment* you're finished, I'll want your help again. There'll be no idleness in this house."

Invigilator of the woodpile. *That* will surely broaden my mind.

"Wabbit!"

Sure enough, there's a rabbit near the open cabin door, nibbling the wilted lettuce Jer left there as bait. He leaps off his stool and starts toward it, but Mr. W catches him by the waist of his britches.

"Hold on, son. You sit and finish your breakfast. Then you ask to be excused. Hear?" He plops Jer back on the stool in front of his toast and eggs.

Jer gapes at me, stunned silent.

I shrug. "You heard him. Eat up."

"Oh, for heaven's sake!" Mrs. D groans. "He's just a little boy! Jer, off you go."

"No," Mr. W says, and he doesn't say it mean but he does say it firm enough that Mrs. D stops halfway to Jer's stool. "This might be the frontier, but there's no reason the boy can't make his manners. Blazes, even the meanest bull cook in the most lawless mining camp north of the Fraser River insisted on *please* and *thank you*."

Mrs. D blinks rapidly. When that look comes on her face, I go right to *yes, ma'am* or *no, ma'am*, but this is Mr. W and he has a point she can't rightly ignore.

"If Jane is responsible for the dishes, Jer needs a chore

or two as well," Mr. W goes on. "He's big enough to fill the woodbox. Don't you think, Jer?"

"He'll get splinters!" Mrs. D cries. "And there are *spiders* in there, and he's still little—"

"I'm a *big* boy," Jer says firmly.

Mr. W points to a crate next to the hearth. "Every time you see the woodbox empty, Jer, go to the shed and bring in wood till it's full. Carry a piece at a time if you need to, but that's your job now. Do you understand?"

Jer crams more eggs in his mouth. I nudge him and whisper, "It's polite to answer when someone asks you a question."

"A'right." Jer wads the rest of his toast into his mouth too. "Wabbit now?"

"It's *May I be excused?*" Mr. W gives Mrs. D a Look, and I squirm a little because I probably should have taught Jer to make his manners better than this. Heaven knows he wouldn't have learned it anywhere else.

"May I be skewsed?" Jer repeats.

"Yes, Jer. Thank you, son."

Mr. W is still chewing his last mouthful when Mrs. D says, "The dishes, Jane," like I might have forgotten in the last two minutes.

It takes three trips to the well to bring the dishes, the draining board, the washrag, the brick of brown soap, and the bag of scouring sand. Mr. W watches me from where he's watering the garden. Any moment now he'll say how I'm not doing it properly or how his mother did it better. Any moment now he'll have a nit to pick.

He doesn't, though. Instead, he glances at Mrs. D sweeping the threshold stone and rolls his eyes, like *she's* the one doing something wrong or silly.

18

A FEW DAYS LATER I'M FINISHING THE BREAKFAST dishes when Mr. W asks if I want to go with him to check the traps.

"Like . . . with animals?" I ask.

Mr. W nods. "Fur fetches a good price in town."

"Jane doesn't know the first thing about traps. Besides, the floor wants a good scrubbing." Mrs. D tries to give Mr. W a Look, but he smiles pleasantly like he doesn't understand.

My knees ache just thinking about being on them all day to wash the floor. Not to mention all the getting up and kneeling it takes to empty the bucket every arm's length when the water gets murky. Also, how the well gets a little farther away with every trip.

"If Jane goes with me, we can check more traps," Mr. W tells her. "If we check all the traps today, we might have enough pelts to trade for that pretty calico you had your eye on."

Jenny and Evie are probably playing hopscotch in the dirt behind Bachelor's Hall. Nell is likely in Mrs. Yesler's parlor drinking tea and chatting about *back East*. Or she's giggling devilishly with Ida as they dare each other to walk past the vicey buildings down on the sawdust.

None of my friends will look at me the same if they know how I spend my days.

Mrs. D purses her lips. She's probably thinking about her own knees, but at length she says, "Yes, that'll be for the best. I'll pack you some dinner to take."

She busies herself with cold biscuits and smoked salmon like the decision's been made, but Mr. W turns to me.

"Jane? You want to go? No skin off my nose if you'd rather scrub floors, but I could use your help."

If my mind will be shrinkened either way, I might as well help Mr. W, who gave me a fish and asks what I think. At the very least I won't have to listen to Mrs. D telling me how I'm scrubbing wrong.

"All right." I try to smile. "I'll go."

Jer looks up. He's halfway under his bed, trying to get Hoss, who skidded all the way to the wall. "I go too."

"Sorry, son," Mr. W replies. "You're too little."

"No, I'm big."

Mrs. D hands me our dinner wrapped in oilcloth. "Charles, you should take Jer, too. Boys need to learn these things. You said as much yourself."

"He wouldn't last the morning," Mr. W says, pleasant but firm. "Both Jane and I will be hauling pelts, so neither of us will be able to carry a tired boy. There'll be plenty of time for him to learn when he's older."

Mrs. D must want her calico, because she doesn't so much as huff. She doesn't make Jer stay inside, though, so he follows us to the shed. Mr. W pulls out a rucksack stained with crusty, dried blood. My stomach lurches, but he's handing it to me and not Jer and he needs my help and it's not scrubbing floors and I can do this.

"Me too." Jer holds out his hands.

"Sorry, son," Mr. W says, ruffling his hair and gently nudging him back to the house. "You can't come with us today. Go help your mama, all right?"

Jer starts howling and sits down hard in the mud outside the shed. I sigh and start to kneel, but Mr. W gently takes my arm and steers me toward the path that takes us toward the privy.

"Let him be upset," Mr. W mutters as we walk. "Let his mother sort it."

"She's hopeless!" I protest, and it's out of my mouth before I realize how impertinent it is. So I rush on, "I mean, she's got what she wants. She's got *everything* she wants. Down to Jer by her side all day, every day. Only he's always too something—too loud, too dirty, too weepy, too sticky. He'll never be exactly what she wants."

Mr. W squints thoughtfully. "It's a hard thing. Realizing that what you want more than anything doesn't really exist. At least not how you pictured it in your head. You convince yourself it's the only thing that'll make you happy. Then you're confronted with absolute proof you'll never have it. Not because you didn't earn it or aren't willing to work for it. You'll never have it, because it just isn't there to be had. By anyone."

"So . . ." I duck under a low limb. "What do you do about it?"

"Well, you could always go to the Fraser River and look for gold," Mr. W says with half a smile.

We come to the first trap, but it's empty. Something's eaten the bait, though, so Mr. W shows me how to hold down the trigger and replace the flake of smoked fish.

The next few traps do have animals in them. Two muskrats, three beavers, and an otter. I feel a little sad for them, but mostly I'm thinking how nice it will be to eat something other than fish and wapatos for every meal.

The sun's high overhead when Mr. W points to a narrow break in the trees. We step onto a sheltered stretch of mud and stumps that opens right onto the lake. It's like the dock, only instead of being surrounded by water, a beach of sorts has been built up over the stumps with dirt and clay and sand. Mr. W calls it the long bank, and he says we're going to skin and dry some of the meat here.

"Watch carefully." Mr. W pulls out a knife the length of his hand. "I'm going to do a few, then it'll be your turn."

The first time I had to wring a chicken's neck, I cried like Jer. My constitution wasn't nearly as sturdy back then.

"All right, but . . ." I study my dirty bare feet under my dirtier skirt. "Maybe this is something you should wait and teach Jer."

Mr. W chuckles. "It's going to be years before Jer is ready to come out with me. You're ready right now. If you're trying to hint that skinning animals isn't for girls, I wish I could take you over to Port Madison and sit you down with Louisa and her sisters. There's also more than one Seattle matron who can make short work of a still-warm otter if her husband's not around."

I must learn to be on the Pacific coast, where girls can keep lighthouses and skin otters and scrub floors and teach school and make socks to sell and chop firewood.

I kneel next to Mr. W. I hope my breakfast stays down.

Mr. W slits and slices, and the beavers and the otter are soon relieved of their pelts. Then it's my turn. I take the limp muskrat he hands me, pull in a deep breath, and cut.

"Like that," Mr. W says. "Good. Now wait for the blood to drain. Remember, you shouldn't puncture any of the organs, because it'll ruin the meat. All right. Slowly there. Well done! You've got it now."

My meat does not look like Mr. W's, all thin strips that can be draped over racks for drying. It looks like meat you'd throw to dogs. I just ruined a perfectly good muskrat, and next time I'll be scrubbing floors for sure.

Mr. W only shrugs. "Don't worry. This is how you learn. We'll take it home, and Mrs. Wright can stew it up. Your pelt isn't so bad for a first try. Here, I'll show you how to flesh it."

Two minutes in, I understand why we remove the lingering shreds of meat from the pelts on the long bank. It's stomach-turning, slimy work. Mr. W explains everything as we do it, how to stretch the skin and how to peg it so it keeps the proper shape. Just like Nell and Flora taught me how to bid and trump at whist.

This is how you learn.

I didn't know how to change a diaper till Jer was born. I couldn't read a word till I went to school, and I couldn't get a stew to thicken till I fumbled in a corn muffin. I didn't know port from starboard till the deckhands on the *Continental* set me straight, and if it weren't for Nell I wouldn't know how to count cards.

Maybe my mind is broader than I thought.

Once all the pelts are curing beneath the canvas shelter, Mr. W and I wash up and eat our dinner. It's peaceful on the lake, and we watch birds glide overhead and otters splash nearby.

It's not a banker's fancy parlor. It's not even a room in a hotel. But it takes a certain kind of clever to make a sturdy shoreline out of stumps and mud when the trees are determined to grow down to and into the waterline all hidden and treacherous.

It takes a certain kind of stubborn to decide something should exist when it's never been there before.

I tear my skirt as I'm climbing off the long bank. Not just a little rip, either. I'm showing the whole world my petticoat past the knee. My legs, too.

But the world right now is just Mr. W and me, and after he finishes flustering and turning red and babbling that maybe I should start wearing britches to do my chores, he puts himself in front of me so there's no one but the birds and deer behind me to stare.

Papa would have been horrified. The Lowell mill girls would have all turned away to spare me the shame. Same with Nell and Flora, the card-room girls, and probably the missuses of Seattle, too.

Out here there's no one to see. This isn't Lowell. It's not New York City. It's not even the Queen City of King County.

When I get back to the cabin, I write a reflection: *This is the Eastside, and birds and deer don't care about things like doors on privies and girls in trousers.*

19

IT'S INDEPENDENCE DAY TODAY, AND WE'RE spending it in Seattle. There's going to be horse racing and speeches and maybe even fireworks.

And my friends. I hope.

The sun rises as Mr. W paddles, and before long we land at the old Indian camp where the trail to town begins. There are other canoes lined up above the waterline, and I can't help but wonder whose they are. I thought we were pretty much the only people on the whole Eastside.

The sun is higher now, and it sends a shaft of light down the mill road and lights up the bay beyond. At the bottom of the hill, through the gap in the big cedars, the streets appear in their angled grid and the white-shiny buildings pop up like mushrooms.

Ahead, Jenny is helping a woman who must be her mother put up a table made of sawhorses. Her green dress isn't stitched up the haunch where she tore it on the long bank, and she's got ribbons on her braids, because it's Seattle and there are no low-hanging brambles to catch and tear them.

Jenny spots me and waves. She waves like it was only yesterday she asked after me at the hotel and we met the others at the old Blaine orchard to watch boats. She waves like it doesn't matter how ragged my hands are.

I turn to Mrs. D. "May I go play with my friends?"

"I want to go wi' Daney," says Jer.

"You may, if you take your brother," Mrs. D replies.

Mr. W fidgets with his hat. "Today's a celebration. We should all enjoy ourselves. I can't see how—"

"Charles, I know you mean well," Mrs. D says to him in a buttery voice, "but you have a lot to learn about children."

He has a lot to learn about Mrs. D, too, but he's got to learn it the same way I did. The same way I learned to skin a muskrat and turn the heel of a sock.

"Yes, ma'am." I take Jer's hand and promise to meet them at sundown on the Occidental's common.

As soon as she and Mr. W are out of sight, I walk Jer real slow past the little cabin the Pollards are renting.

Sure enough, Jimmie Lincoln is playing in the yard, and both he and Jer squeal with joy when they see each other. They rush to the fence and reach their small hands through the slats, trying to hug.

Mrs. Pollard invites me in for a mug of tea, and considering I'm about to ask a big favor, I don't think I ought to refuse. When she hands me a plate of butter cookies, I'm glad I didn't.

"I don't mind at all, lamb," Mrs. Pollard says as we finally get up from her hearth bench. "Keeps Jimmie out of my hair. You can come get your brother whenever you like."

Jer waves a happy farewell as I bang through the Pollards' gate and down the muddy street. Jenny's mother has spread a pretty cloth on their table and put out a tempting plate of strawberries. Evie's joined them, and she and Jenny are arguing.

". . . dolls, of all things!" Jenny rolls her eyes. "We can play dolls anytime. It's Independence Day, for heaven's sake!"

"I like playing dolls," Evie replies. "Besides, the celebration isn't even starting till—Jane!"

She gives me a hug, then holds me at arm's length. Jenny does too, and both of them start exclaiming how good it is to see me and how much they've missed my company.

"You like playing dolls, right?" Evie asks, giving Jenny a Look.

"Jane probably doesn't have a moment for us today," Jenny teases. "She's managed to escape the wilderness and she likely wants to visit with Miss Stewart and the other young ladies."

Jenny's smiling, but there's a catch in her voice. She means it. These girls have missed me. They think I'm the one who's beyond their company, not the other way around.

"Of course I want to play dolls," I say, and I nudge them both cheerfully like Nell might. "Jenny can run home and get hers, and Evie and I will find Inez and Madge."

It's still hard for me to just walk through Evie's front door. Her papa is a ship's captain, and their house is so grand it makes me want to go around back like a servant. Evie's room is spotless as always. There are two windows with yellow gingham curtains and a bed covered in quilts and a tall, graceful wardrobe.

Before I can even ask, Evie opens the fancy sea chest at the foot of her brass bedstead and holds her old rag doll out with a smile that says, *I'm sorry she's so shabby*. Evie's rag doll is not made of rags at all. She's got a muslin body, braided yarn hair, and a tiny pinafore made out of calico that's newer than the dress I'm wearing now.

Soon, Jenny's clattering up the stairs, and we're all gathered on Evie's rug. The four of them have dolls with china heads and party dresses, and I have Felicity with her flat-stitched hands and feet. You can tell she's a doll, but she's definitely not like the others.

The dolls go to a fancy ball and dance with handsome princes, then they go back to their finishing school. They're always together wherever they go, and they're the best of friends, even Felicity, who until recently had been forgotten in Evie's sea chest.

After a while it starts being fun. We make it fun, all of us together. There are lots of things the dolls could do and adventures they could go on. If only I could come back to Evie's every day and the five of us could play this game forever.

When the dolls are asleep, I ask Evie for a drink of water. She walks me downstairs to the bucket and dipper, and while we're passing through the kitchen, there's a knock at the door. Mrs. Mason answers, and it's an Indian woman selling fresh fish.

"*Ik-tah kunsih?*" Mrs. Mason asks. They go back and forth awhile before she trades the woman some eggs for two big salmon.

If Mrs. Mason in her back East dresses and rosewater

perfume speaks Chinook, it really does mean everyone knows some.

Back upstairs I pick up Felicity and ask, "Do they teach Chinook in school here? When there is school, I mean."

Evie shakes her head. "Chinook is something you just pick up. Even me, and I didn't grow up speaking it like Madge and Inez and Jenny did. You'll learn."

This is how you learn.

I stand Felicity on her flour-sack feet. "What if the dolls meet a prince at the next ball, and he only speaks Chinook? Then you all can help me help Felicity talk to him."

Madge purses her lips. "No one *only* speaks Chinook. All right, though. Hyacinth will help Felicity talk to Prince . . . Pierre."

Felicity has a nice conversation with Prince Pierre, who is played quite ably by a dishrag bound with string to make it shaped like a boy. They talk about how much things cost and where things are, and by the time we hear the band start up, I can confidently ask people's names, tell them my own, and say *please* and *thank you*.

My mind is a little broader already.

The streets are much busier now that the sun is higher. The band is playing on Yesler's Pavilion down by the wharf. Houses are all hung with bunting, and most of the stores have tables out front where they're selling lemonade and sweets and ale.

Kids are everywhere. They're racing through the streets shouting and cheering and chasing dogs and losing their hats and bonnets. Indian kids are running around as well as white kids, and there are even a few small Chinese boys who have pigtails just like their papas.

It makes no sense that there's no school here. There are plenty of children.

I spot Ida and Nell walking with two young men. How boring. Nell should come join us. We've got big plans, starting with trying to sweet-talk Mr. Plummer into giving us lemonade without handing over a nickel none of us have. I'm still not happy they didn't tell me there were no schools, but my head may well have been turned too, had I gotten all that attention just for setting foot in town.

Nell doesn't look bored, though. She looks happy. She's twirling a parasol and grinning that old saucy cards-in-the-necessary smile.

I might not be old enough for courting, but I know now's not the time to rush up and embrace her. So I just wave. Nell doesn't stand on such formality, though, and plows over to me like a ship under sail.

"Isn't he handsome?" Nell whispers in my ear. "He's

also a total bore! Looks like I'm at the Carrs' a little longer. Not that they mind. Nor do I. I love them. They're teaching me to mend nets. Fishing nets! Can you believe?"

I can, actually. Ostrich-plume, flouncy-skirt Nell Stewart, queen of the last-minute trick, is learning to mend fishing nets in yet another family she's found herself part of.

"Your friends are waiting." Nell nudges me toward Evie and the others, who are staring like fish caught in her new-mended nets. "Go on, I'll catch up with you later. I have to let ol' Snoremaker down gently."

Nell squeezes my arm and swishes off. My Seattle friends are still exclaiming over how exciting courting must be, when there's a gunshot.

I flinch, but Inez squeals, "Oh! They must be racing on Front Street already."

Evie trots a few paces ahead. "We should go watch my brother. He's got a chestnut gelding that's so quick off the line it's *breathtaking*."

"I'm going to run over to Mrs. Pollard's," I say. "I have to check on my brother and make sure he isn't driving her to distraction. I'll meet you there."

Jenny takes my elbow. "We'll all go."

So we do. All of us together.

Jer is napping when we stop by. Mrs. Pollard says he's

been no trouble at all, and we girls should go have fun and eat plenty of oysters for her.

I make a face—everyone here can't get enough of those slimy rock-slugs but I can't stand the *sight* of them—and Mrs. Pollard laughs as we plunge out of her gate and down the hill toward the bay.

The horse racing is most exciting. We shout our lungs raw for Evie's brother, but he comes a distant third to Stephen Collins's glossy black mare. Jenny's mother treats us all to strawberries and cream, courtesy of the Ladies' Mite Society.

We're sitting in the shade outside the old blockhouse waiting for the next race to start when Mrs. D darts around the corner like she's looking to hide. Mr. Mercer is right behind her. He puts himself in her path and stabs his finger into his palm as if he's making a point. Mrs. D lifts her chin, but doesn't say a thing. Her cheeks are bright red. Mr. Mercer gives a massive fed-up sigh, then stalks off.

That's likely for the best. As far as I can tell, she'd still as soon kill him with her bare hands.

Mrs. D leans against the side of the blockhouse and lets out a long breath like a bull when he's angry. Then she spots me. I give a little halfhearted wave, but her eyes drop to my side and her whole face goes panicky.

"Jane? Oh my heavens, where is he? Where's Jer? Why aren't you *watching* him? He could be trampled or drowned or—"

"It's all right," I cut in. "Ma'am! Jer's playing with Jimmie Lincoln. Mrs. Pollard has him. It's *fine*."

I know full well it's rude to interrupt, and she's bound to give me an earful, but she's so screechy and terrified I feel honest-to-goodness bad for her as she fights to catch her breath and presses both hands to her chest.

Mr. W comes up behind her and gently squeezes her shoulders. "See? Jane has it all in hand. Jer's bound to have a better time playing with a boy his own age than tagging after his big sister."

Mrs. D busies herself brushing dirt off her sleeve. If she gets upset at me for doing something nice for Jer— even if it happens to be nice for me as well—she'll be the one to look the fool.

"Well, then," Mrs. D says, "I'll go check on him, shall I? Make sure he's not too much trouble for Mrs. Pollard?"

"Yes, ma'am, only I just—"

She's already bustling up the hill, clutching her hat with one hand. Mr. W smiles in a what-can-I-do? sort of way and follows.

I know what's coming. I turn to my friends and say, "Let's go back to Evie's and send the dolls on a sea voyage." It will take Mrs. D a long time to find me there.

"No thanks," Jenny says. "I want to see the next race."

"Me too," adds Inez. "Everyone says Mr. Ling's colt can't be beat."

Sure enough, before the next set of horses is even lined up, Mrs. D comes back to Front Street towing Jer by the hand. Mr. W trails her, holding a bowl of strawberries and cream and looking like he could use a long drink of water.

"See?" Mrs. D sits Jer beside me on the bench, then pulls the bowl of berries out of Mr. W's hands and thrusts it into Jer's. "Jer had had enough of Jimmie Lincoln, and it wouldn't be right to keep Mrs. Pollard from enjoying Independence Day, would it?"

She's giving me a Look, so I know the right answer.

"No, ma'am."

"Good." Mrs. D nods like everything is finally in order. "We're beholden enough without owing Mrs. Pollard, too. I'm away to Mrs. Grinold's. There's a lot of horses out today, Jane. Do please keep a firm eye on him."

Then she's off, still holding down her hat, in the direction Mr. Mercer didn't go.

"I hope she can have your pardon," Mr. W mumbles to me. "Asa Mercer had the bad taste to confront her about money. In public, too."

Madge and Inez are studying their bowls. Jenny is

picking at a loose thread on her sleeve, and Evie is swinging her legs. They are all trying to pretend my stepmother
didn't just have the bad taste to confront me about something that was already taken care of in a way that gave
everyone something they wanted.

"Jer wanted to see the mill." Mr. W is pink from the
sun and the walk and probably Mrs. D, although he'd
never admit it. "I don't mind taking him over there.
Seems like you're having a good time with your friends."

I hand my bowl to Inez. "No, I'd better take him.
Mrs. Dem—Wright won't like it if she finds out I *imposed*
on you."

"Shall we let Jer decide?" Mr. W asks.

I open my mouth to say, *Jer's too little to decide anything. He won't care so long as his belly is full of strawberries
and there's someone to put him on their shoulders.*

"Mill! Mill! Bzzzzzzzzzzz!" Jer sings, like it's the most
ordinary thing in the world to just decide things and
expect grown-ups to listen.

Jer's never had a father. Not one he remembers, anyway. This way is better, I think. This way, he's always had
an Uncle Charlie, just like he's always had a Mama and
a Daney. By the time Jer's old enough to reckon what he
doesn't have, he'll be more than happy with what he's got
in front of him.

WE MAKE IT BACK TO THE CABIN JUST AS THE last bit of evening is turning into night. Jer is hard asleep, and he looks like a baby again as Mr. W carries him against his shoulder all the way from Seattle to the camp landing and then up the lake trail to the cabin. Mrs. D takes Jer inside while I help Mr. W look in on the chickens and garden.

"You're quiet," Mr. W says as I haul up the water bucket. "Didn't you have a good time in town? I thought girls squealed and chattered and . . . such."

"I did. I reckon."

Mr. W peers at me. "You reckon?"

Mrs. D hates it when I *whine*. But this is Mr. W, who took Jer to see the mill and thinks nothing of giving me chores like cutting kindling and skinning animals as if they're ordinary.

"I miss them, is all." My throat gets stoppery. "My friends. Evie Mason and Jenny McConaha and the Denny girls."

"You got to spend the whole day with them." Mr. W sounds puzzled.

"Yes, and tomorrow the four of them will go to Evie's and play dolls, or they'll go to the woods fort or pick flowers in Mrs. Denny's garden, and here I'll be. Just me and the trees until who knows when. Next Independence Day, for all I know."

Mr. W pours water into two waiting buckets. "I didn't think of that."

"Of what?"

"That whoever came to live here with me might miss town society." He smiles sadly. "I couldn't think of living in that nest of vipers. Self-important, self-interested blowhards, the lot of them, who couldn't agree a quarter's two bits. They'd just see a quarter and come to blows over whose it was."

I take one of the buckets and start pouring it in the furrow between rows of corn.

"Your stepmother knew what she was taking on," Mr. W adds. "She couldn't wait to be away from a place where no one could talk about anything but how courageous and stouthearted and precious the Mercer Girls were. I thought she told you we'd be out here. I thought you'd know."

I can see her considering such a plan. I can even see her shouting it in a fit of rage. For her to actually quit Seattle with clear and open eyes—Mrs. D has a sturdier constitution than I thought.

Mr. W refills my bucket, and together we water the garden. Bucket by bucket, row by row. It's soothing, my feet in the dirt and birds chirring in the falling daylight. Already it feels like a normal chore, like checking the traps or grubbing stumps. Everything is greening up big and leafy and spry, the turnips bushy and the squash twining everywhere and a mess of carrots almost springing from the ground behind the deer fence.

"It's not that I don't like it here," I say quietly, "but I wish I could see my friends more often."

Mr. W nods. He doesn't say I'm being silly. He doesn't roll his eyes and tell me I'm just trying to shirk my chores. So I keep talking. I tell him how Nell and Flora and I had the run of the *Continental*, how we bounced like spinning tops from the card room to the hurricane deck, and how we wept to part company. How Evie came right up to me that first day like I was as good as anyone else and how surprised my Seattle friends were to see me today, like the Eastside might as well be back East.

We haul and dump buckets. Mr. W doesn't lie or soothe. He just keeps nodding till I'm out of things to say and it's too dark to see.

Later, I set a candle on the ledge in the privy and open my little book. *Sometimes when there's nothing helpful to say, the best thing you can do is listen.*

Mr. W and I are burning a stump today, which is also becoming an ordinary chore on account of the number of stumps we make while we cut down winter firewood and grow our clearing that much bigger as we do it.

"Hollow out a hole in the side of the stump and we'll light a fire in it." He hands me a hatchet. "I'm going to cut from the other side."

As we're chopping, Mr. W clears his throat. "I've been thinking about what you said. About missing your friends. How would you fancy having your own canoe?"

My hatchet goes *kerthunk* so hard I struggle to free it. "I . . . *what?*"

"Like mine," Mr. W says, and he's all stammery again, the way he gets when he's nervous. "Only yours. Made for you, so it's not too heavy for you to pull."

"But that . . . I'm not . . . is that *allowed?*"

Mr. W snorts a laugh. "Allowed? Of course it's allowed! You think anyone gets anywhere *walking* in these parts? The lake's the road here, or the bay, or Puget Sound. A dock's the same as a front door."

When I was very small, I'd look out my window in the farmhouse and imagine where the road went that ribboned past our door and out of sight. Lowell had a crazy quilt of streets and alleys, and New York was Lowell but ten times taller, forty times busier, and a hundred times dirtier.

Roads, always. Cobbles and more cobbles or hard-packed dirt.

A canoe would change everything.

I could finish my chores and walk down the lake trail to the dock. To my own canoe, where I'd climb in and paddle till I got to the camp landing, then it'd be a manageable walk to Seattle and my friends.

Mrs. D would never allow it.

Mrs. D isn't the only person who can allow me to do things now.

I grin at Mr. W across the stump. "I'd love one! Only . . . we don't have money for a canoe. Do we?"

"We don't need money." Mr. W holds up his hatchet. "Just time and sweat. You're going to make your canoe yourself."

A day goes by, then two. Mr. W and I burn stumps and check the traps, and there's no more talk of a canoe.

My wooden fish weighs down my pocket along with my hopscotch stone and my shiny blue bead from Rio. I rub it constantly while I water the garden and gather the eggs and remind Jer to fill the woodbox.

On the third day, I'm kneading bread when Mr. W calls for me from the top of the lake trail. I turn the dough over to Mrs. D—she's less than happy—and find him on the edge of the clearing where we've left the biggest, toughest cedars alone. There's an Indian man with him, and they're squinting at the trees.

"This is Lawrence," Mr. W says. "He's going to help with the canoe."

I'm all kinds of curious about Lawrence. Perhaps he's a friend or maybe a relation of Mr. W's old sweetheart. I also know it's rude to pry, so I just smile and say, "*Kla-ho'w-ya?*" which I hope means *How do you do?* like Felicity said to Prince Pierre and not something silly like *Are there fish in your britches?*

"*Kloshe.*" Over his shoulder Lawrence is carrying a rucksack that clanks like it's full of tools.

Mr. W waits, but when I hold out my hands palms-up to show I'm out of Chinook, he chuckles. "He said he's doing well enough." Mr. W nudges me. "See? I knew you'd pick up some words. Shall we get started?"

The first thing we do is choose the right tree. Actually,

Lawrence and Mr. W decide on the tree. They hammer in the springboards and chop from either side, and it's down by the time Mrs. D has dinner ready. Jer is so used to trees falling that he knows to run into the house or next to the garden when Mr. W calls a warning.

The tree is bigger than I thought it would be. Lawrence marks it in two places with a stick he blackens in a stump fire.

"That's where we'll cut," Mr. W explains. "We've got to make the canoe long enough that it balances, but not so long you can't pull it. You ready to saw?"

After all that work on the woodpile, I'm decent with a handsaw. Mr. W does one cut and I do the other. The length of cedar we end up with is about twice my height and as thick as my arm is long.

"Tomorrow you'll take the bark off," Mr. W says. "For the rest of today, I'll be fishing with Lawrence. You've got firewood to cut and stack, and see if you can't chop the burned part out of that stump and set it smoldering again."

Split, carry, stack. We'll be warm all winter because of me. My hands have long since gone blistery, then rough. It's not like when they were washwater-wrinkled, though. Now they feel powerful.

As the sun is going down, I write a reflection: *Being*

the invigilator of the woodpile takes both a broad mind and a sturdy constitution.

Several days later Mr. W hands me a tool that looks like a knife blade set between two wooden handles. "This is an adze. Here's how to work it."

He puts the blade against the canoe-tree, just under the bark, and pulls back in one long, even swipe. A curl of bark follows. When I try it, the blade catches and jutters, and I nearly take my thumb off.

"Push down while you're pulling back." Mr. W flutters his hands near mine on the tool like he wants to help but isn't sure what I'll say. "Like that. Exactly. There you go!"

A stubby curl of bark comes off the log. It's the length of my hand and nowhere near the sleek slice Mr. W made.

"Try again," he says. "Make it as smooth as you can. You'll get it."

Once I've made a few cuts, Mr. W goes to check on the stumps we're burning. On the other side of the clearing, Mrs. D hangs laundry on the washing line, pegs to the seams, stiff with starch. Just the way she likes it. Just the way I struggle to make it and have to redo again and again till it's right.

"Well done!" Mr. W peers over my shoulder. "Keep that up, all right? Try to take the bark off as evenly as you can, but don't worry if it's not just so. I'm going to check the traps."

All the rest of the day I take uneven hacks of bark off the log while Mr. W skins three muskrats and a beaver. By afternoon my pieces are longer and smoother, and I don't have to go back over the log with the blade to even it. I shave bark the next day too, all day in the rain, and by suppertime my curls of bark are so long and delicate that Jer starts collecting them and hanging them on bushes like horses' tails.

When all the bark is off, Lawrence comes by to show us how to shape the bow and stern. He gestures with the hatchet and talks in Chinook, but I don't know enough words to follow.

"He's saying you should be gentle," Mr. W explains. "You can always take more off. You can't add it back on."

Lawrence comes up the lake trail every few days to discuss the angle of the sides or the shape of the bottom. After he's gone, Mr. W tells me more stories about the Fraser River gold rush.

We can't work on the canoe all day—more's the pity—but we do some every day before we cut down trees and burn stumps and tend the garden and check the traps. I forget what it's like to wear a dress. I keep a pail of water by the door so I can wash my feet before going into the cabin.

In the falling daylight, I write a reflection: *Ordinary is in the eye of the beholder*.

When the canoe is finally the right shape, Mr. W and I heave it over with something called a come-along. It sits there heavy and lumpen, looking like a canoe that's been filled with sand.

"She's lovely!" Mr. W grins. "What do you think, Jane?"

"Um . . . it's pointy at the ends."

What I'm not saying is that the thing in the clearing might be pointy at the ends, but it's still pretty much a log. It's going to take—*forever* to hollow all that out chip by chip with a hatchet. I'll be as old as Nell by the time it's lakeworthy. Perhaps even as old as Mrs. D.

Only, I don't want to hurt Mr. W's feelings when he's put as much sweat as I have into this so-called canoe. Good thing I have a whist face convincing enough for the card rooms of San Francisco.

Mr. W only smiles and nods at the hatchet I'm holding. "Chip out a trough a hand wide and a finger deep right down the middle."

When it's done, he tells me to collect rocks about the size of my fist and put them into the hottest stump fire. Once they've heated, I pour water in the little trough and lay the hot rocks in one at a time with a big pair of rusty blacksmith tongs.

"Now we let it simmer, just like a stew," Mr. W says.

We go check the traps, and by the time we come back, the wood simply *peels* away. We slice as much as we can before the wood cools, but we get enough that I realize there won't be any painstaking, hand-blistering chipping. We just need to have the patience to keep up this rocks-and-water routine for days and days.

While we're setting the rocks back in the fire, Jer comes over. He's holding his favorite stick in one hand and a baked wapato in the other. "Can I help?"

"Sorry," I tell him, "but this is hot and—"

"Sure, son," Mr. W cuts in. "Find us some smooth rocks to put in the fire. Big ones. Like those."

"A'right!" Jer crams his wapato into his mouth and rushes off to the end of the clearing closest to the lake path. In moments he's back, and he drops a rock at our feet and grins up at Mr. W. "Here y'are, Daddy!"

Mr. W flusters. Harder than he usually does. He's got the biggest, silliest grin on his face too. Bigger and sillier than when he said *I do* in the white church.

Then he pets Jer's hair gently and says, "Th-thank you, son. Go get some more. As many as you can."

Jer beams and hustles off.

Mr. W glances at me sidelong, like he wants to beg my pardon and isn't sure how. Or perhaps like he thinks he should beg my pardon but really doesn't want to.

I reckon I see why, but Papa was dead months before Jer was born. He'd want Jer to have a father. A boy needed his father from the beginning, Papa said, but girls didn't need their fathers till they started courting. The farm needed him more than I did, so he was always behind the plow or the harrow or in the tavern for a mug of ale and a song or two, and the wheat grew up tall and strong and not at all lonely.

I look down at the stump fire full of rocks soaking up heat. At Mr. W's boots and my own, and beyond at the canoe we're making, both of us together, with our own hands.

"I'm glad," I say. "Jer needs a father that's here. Not one that's passed on and can't do anything for him."

"I never thought I'd actually have a family of my own." Mr. W makes a vague gesture at his potato-shaped self. "Sometimes it's hard to think of you and Rose and Jer as my family. You were all together for so long, then along I came. Grafted on."

I peer at him. He can't really think *he's* the one who doesn't belong.

"We are a family, though," Mr. W goes on, like just saying it makes it so, "and I don't exactly know how to . . . do that. How to be a father. Mine . . . taught me what *not* to do. The best thing I can think to do for you and Jer is what I wish my father—or anyone—would have done for me. And that's show me things. Anything. *Everything*. It's bone-tiring to learn every single lesson the hard-knock way."

"Like a sea dad," I say. "That's how you learn things on a ship. The deckhands on the *Continental* told me that. Because so many of them run away to sea when they're just boys, the older sailors show them how to climb rigging and move sails and such. Different than their actual fathers, of course, but like fathers when it comes to seafaring. It's why the deckhands were so willing to show us things."

Mr. W smiles as he nudges the rocks with a blackened poker. "Must have been a marvelous trip."

"Only, I reckon you'd be our homestead dad," I go on thoughtfully, because there's so many things that make our homestead go—from cedars to traps to drying racks down on the long bank—that Mr. W is an expert on and broadening my mind with.

It's only when Mr. W goes from flustery to completely still that I realize what I said. He's standing in this awkward frozen way, like if he makes the slightest wrong move, I'll take it back.

I don't want to take it back.

All those months ago in New York I hoped Mrs. D would meet a man who stepped straight out of Mr.

Mercer's pamphlet and gave her whatever she wanted so she'd be happy.

Mr. W did one better, though. He stepped out of *my* pamphlet. The one I made with my own hands.

"That's all right, isn't it?" I ask quietly. "I mean, I had a papa. He's gone, though, and right now I could really use a dad."

Mr. W comes around the fire to stand beside me. He shifts like he thinks to hug me but isn't sure if it's right. "Can I tell you something? I'm not sure I'll say it properly, but here goes. A lot of men want sons—and I'm glad of Jer, I really am—but I always thought a daughter would be better. With a daughter, you can just enjoy her company. You're not worried about . . . helping her become a man. Because she doesn't need that from you. She just needs you to be a good man. That's something I know I can do."

Jer runs up, a rock in each hand, grinning so big you'd think every carriage in the whole of back East was parked right in front of him.

My brother is easy to love. Sweet and helpful and mostly sunny-natured. Healthy and strong. Everyone's honeydarling.

I never thought for a moment there could be a downside to being a boy, that I might have something he didn't just because of who I am.

"More rocks, Daddy?" Jer throws down the ones he's got.

"Yes, please," Mr. W says, big and cheerful, to cover up the catch in his voice.

"Yeah," I add, "Dad and I need as many rocks as you can find for the canoe."

Even though Mr. W—Dad—and I spend the rest of the day grubbing stumps and skinning a particularly smelly raccoon, he grins the whole time, big and silly and perfectly happy.

So do I.

Because if I have a dad instead of an Uncle Charlie, instead of a Mr. W, my ramshackle family just got a little more sturdy.

THE CANOE IS FINALLY FINISHED! LAWRENCE kept finding problems with the keel or uneven places in the thickness that would make it wobble and maybe flip over. The cedar cross braces we chose were the wrong length, and we weren't seasoning the wood properly. Finally, though, he runs his hands over bow and stern and sides and nods in his polite, easygoing way.

"*Kloshe kopa nika*," Lawrence says, which Dad tells me is high praise indeed.

The canoe is a lovely, shiny red-brown, and about a finger-length in thickness, which feels like a lot of wood to have under you and at the same time not enough.

My canoe. The canoe I built, me and my sturdy constitution and Lawrence and my dad.

We portage it from the clearing down the lake path. The day is bright and sunny, almost Mediterranean, and the lake ripples out crisp and blue and perfect. The water level's down far enough to expose the stump dock, so Dad and I carry the canoe right out to the end of it and lower it into the water.

Before he'll even hand me a paddle, Dad insists I learn to right myself. That means getting back in my canoe if it tips over.

It's exactly as terrifying and impossible as it sounds, but I spend the rest of the afternoon tumbling out of that dratted canoe next to the dock, where Dad can fish me out before I drown. By sundown I can hit the water, thrash a few times, clumsily put my canoe on its keel, and crawl back in. Dad makes me do it twice in a row before pronouncing me seaworthy.

Even though I'm soaking wet and swaying on my feet, he gives me an awkward hug across the shoulders.

Even though I'm soaking wet and swaying on my feet, I hug him back.

The next day Dad and I go down the lake trail and find the stump dock just peeking above the waterline. My small canoe is tied up peaceably next to Dad's big one. A little boat family. Today I'm finally going to get on the water.

"A canoe's not exactly complicated." Dad grunts as he kneels and gentles the stern against the dock. "You've just got to keep your weight centered and not make any sudden movements. Hop in."

I don't exactly *hop*, but I do scrabble and scrape my way in and kneel just before the aft cross brace, where Lawrence showed me to. The canoe shifts under me, but Dad is holding it steady.

It's nice, once you get used to the strangeness. Like most things, I reckon, if you consider how *strange* doesn't necessarily mean *bad*.

I squint up at him, one hand to my eyes. "Aren't you getting in?"

Dad shakes his head. "That's the whole point, isn't it? You going places on your own?"

"Wait. No. I can't . . . I don't know anything about canoes!"

"Weren't you left to take care of Jer single-handed when he was just a few weeks old and you were only nine?"

"Well . . . yes. Because I had to, Mrs. D—"

"Did you know anything about babies? How to change them or when to feed them or how to hold them? Did you know how to manage a fire? Or everything it took to keep house?"

I didn't. I hadn't.

This is how you learn.

Right now Evie is playing dolls in her perfect room. Madge and Inez are in their cousins' woods fort. Nell is wandering the Blaine orchard with some new young man. Or mending nets with the Carrs, who love her.

They're all just across the lake. Not a one of them cares what my hands look like.

Dad hands me an oar. "Use the handle end to push off the dock. Otherwise you'll blunt the tip. Make sure you pull on both sides or you'll go in circles."

"Pull?"

"You don't paddle a canoe. You pull it."

I wobble at first. Considerably. Then I work out how to hold my body still and use only my arms. I pull past the dock and up the bank, then back. The green-black water slides past and drips from my oar and catches the sun like a sheet of diamonds.

The lake is simply glorious.

"You think you've got it?" Dad calls as I'm pulling past the dock a fourth time.

"I think so!"

"Good," he shouts. "Then head over to Seattle and pick up some flour and oatmeal. Mr. Pinkham will give you credit."

I freeze, my oar dripping into the lake. "What—now?"

"No time like the present."

"What if I get lost? What if I fall in? What if—"

"I doubt you'll get lost," Dad cuts in. "The Sawgrass camp landing is hard to miss if you paddle west and aim straight. Coming home—you've got a point there. I'll tie some red cloth to this tree so you'll recognize our dock. If you capsize, don't panic. Right your canoe and climb back in and bail the water out. Like you did all day yesterday."

I rest my oar across the canoe and glide. Hardly anyone lives on the Eastside. Neither white people nor Indians. I could pull around forever.

Then Dad calls, "I'll tell Mrs. Wright you won't be back in time to help with the washing."

I can hear the wink in his voice even this far out. I raise my oar to say *thank you*, then turn my bow and start pulling.

I steer toward a stretch of gravel that I'm fairly sure is the camp landing, and as I get nearer, I recognize one old tree with its tangle of roots in the air. I splash into the shallows and drag my canoe up past the waterline like I've seen Dad do.

At the top of the trail I look down over the landing and across the lake. The green of the trees and the blue of the sky and the gray-dark of the water and the brown of the pale, stripped-down trunks that wash up along the shore—they're pretty in a way I never thought to look for. Everything smells crisp and clean, and the wind hushes and rushes like a lullaby.

I compose a reflection in my head: *Timber is not as irritating as it first appears.*

The sun is high, but not overhead. There's time to have tea with Nell and maybe sneak in a hand of whist if Ida and Julia aren't busy. There's also time to send the dolls on that sea voyage or even play sea voyage ourselves in the woods fort, before I'll need to get the dry goods and head home.

Except Mrs. Carr says Nell has a *social engagement* and there's no telling when she'll be back.

There's no answer at Evie's house. Jenny's mother says she's gone to school, but that can't be right, and I don't want to call Mrs. McConaha a liar. Madge and Inez live a ways outside town, and I don't want to spend my precious day in Seattle walking when I can't be sure they'll be home either.

There are new hats in the millinery's window, new copies of the *Puget Sound Weekly*, and gleaming new stoves in Mr. Plummer's store, but no sign of my friends anywhere.

I end up in front of Pinkham's General Store, so I might as well get the dry goods. Mr. Pinkham is out for the day. His shop boy is manning the counter, and he's reluctant to give me goods on credit even though he knows I'm friends with Ida and also that Mr. Pinkham wants to be more than friends with Ida.

"All right," the shop boy finally says, "but you tell Mr. Wright he'll need to pay part of this reckoning next time he's in."

The shop boy weighs out some flour and oatmeal, and of course I didn't bring any bags or baskets with me. He gives me an extra flour sack, but it's another penny. I stand there in my dress with the big mended tear up the haunch that's also too small for me, except I didn't notice it was too small till today because I hardly wear it anymore, and all at once I know why Dad didn't want to come.

He knew he'd have to pay the bill, so he sent me because Ida is my friend.

"Thank you, sir," I mumble as I take the dry goods. I'm not embarrassed by needing credit. Heaven knows we wouldn't have eaten in Lowell without it. But Dad could at least have warned me.

I go past the Carr house again and spot Nell out back pegging laundry to the line. When she sees me, she drops a petticoat and rushes toward me.

"Jane! My dearest one!" Nell takes my hands in hers, then holds me at arm's length. "Heavens, that dress! If that's what a girl is reduced to when she's homesteading, the West will wither right on the vine."

Then she slaps her hands over her mouth. "Oh glory! How terribly rude of me. I do beg your pardon. You must feel bad enough about it already."

I look down at myself. My feet are bare, and I can walk over pine needles without even flinching. There are faint bloodstains on my hem from that first day on the long bank when I made hash of that poor muskrat. My hands are covered in healed-over calluses and filled with little cuts where I took out cedar splinters with Dad's jackknife.

I couldn't do any of that in the lavender muslin rig Nell's got on.

"I don't feel bad about it at all," I tell her, and I mean it.

Nell pats my arm. "Of course, dear heart. Of course you don't, but surely you'll let me lend you a dress to wear to Ida's wedding."

"Ida's getting married?"

"How can you be surprised?" Nell giggles. "Albert Pinkham's been sweet on her since she landed."

I'm not surprised. Not really. Mostly, I hope Mr. Mercer was the first one they told, because it would serve him right to know Ida decided to marry someone who didn't pay him one thin dime.

"It's going to be lovely." Nell reaches into the basket

for another peg. "There'll be flowers and cake and they're getting Mr. Johnson to play the melodeon. The wedding's a week from tomorrow. You have to come!"

"I'll ask my dad," I reply, because I already know what Mrs. D will say. "I'll do my best."

"The kids at her school are planning some sort of trick," Nell goes on. "Even though it's only been a few weeks, they—"

"Wait, what?" I cut in. "What school?"

Nell busies herself pegging a stocking and not looking at me.

That must be where Madge and Inez and Evie are right now. Where *Jenny* is right now, just like her mother told me. They're in school and I'm *missing* it.

"Ida's been holding a school," Nell finally replies in the same reluctant way Elizabeth told me about Violet's birthday party a week after it happened.

"Why didn't she tell me?" I ask. "Why didn't *you* tell me?"

Nell smiles in a belly-pain way. "Ida didn't want a scene. I didn't want you to feel left out on top of being hauled out to the middle of nowhere with no one for company but the harpy."

"A scene?" I repeat, but I know exactly what she means. There would have been a scene too, the moment

Mrs. D got so much as a whisper of either cost or charity.

I'm inclined to make a scene right now. One where I screech at Nell for deciding something for me instead of helping me.

"Is anyone else going to start a school?" I ask wearily. "I won't say you told."

Nell squints. "Mr. Mercer was going to conduct a session up at the university, but he married Annie Stephens and they left town in a most unseemly hurry. Something about a lawsuit by some California miner. I can name at least a dozen bachelors in a day's worth of paddling who'd like a piece of that scoundrel's hide, so it's probably for the best that he went. Both for him and for Annie. Could you help me hang these sheets?"

I climb over the fence and help Nell peg the sheets to the line. I never knew Annie that well. She was friendly to everyone but kept to herself, neither flirting with officers nor playing whist with us. She spent most of her time on the *Continental* quietly sewing on the promenade deck.

I hope at least *she* gets what she expects from Mr. Mercer.

The mill's noon whistle blows, and as the workers troop toward the cookhouse, Mr. Yesler steps onto the porch with his thumbs behind his suspenders to watch them come in.

Nell whips a handkerchief repeatedly at him. "Jane! Seeing that old pinchpenny makes me think how Ida's always on about the ruinous amount of rent he wants for the building she's in now. Which reminds me that I heard one of the girls who came with Mr. Mercer's first expedition is thinking about teaching classes up at the university, because she can't afford Ida's building. So there you are!"

Nell's too bluff and cheerful. She didn't intend to tell me. She has Opinions about how likely it is I'll make it across the lake to school every day, and she knows what it is to have a less-than-reliable guardian.

She knows about my promise, though. Promises mean something to Nell Stewart.

I start pegging clothes like a whirlwind. I hang two shirts to Nell's one and all but fly through the stockings. Then I promise to wear whatever she wants to Ida's wedding, and I'm through the Carrs' gate and hurrying uphill.

I thought to wait around till my friends were out of school, but I'm not in the humor for more excuses. Any one of them could have told me too. Instead, I follow Third Avenue till it becomes something of a bumpy wagon track that winds up and up toward the university.

Up on a knoll the main building stands white and beautiful with its fancy columns and bell tower. It looks out of place, like it blew in from the capital, and the picket fence around it is meant to trap it here.

A building this grand—and probably this expensive—should be bustling. Instead, it's silent.

A young lady is sitting on the porch, reading a book. A young lady with piled hair and a sweeping gray dress who looks like she could step into a game of whist with my *Continental* friends.

"Good afternoon!" I'm way too loud for this quiet place, especially in front of someone trying to read, but I plunge on, "Say, this is the university, right?"

The girl slides her finger into her book and peers up at me. "Yes. For all the good it's doing anyone." She talks a shade too loud and directs most of her statement at the building over her shoulder instead of at me.

"Go home, Miss Baker," a man's voice calls from somewhere inside. He sounds annoyed and weary, like he's been at something unpleasant all day.

She snickers and settles herself against the porch beam. She clearly doesn't intend to do as she's told.

"I'm Jane." I edge toward her hopefully. "Is it true you're opening a school?"

"Nettie." She smiles and holds out a hand, which I shake in what I hope is a grown-up way. "I was told I could teach school, but when I got here, there weren't any."

I snort softly. It's cold comfort to know Mr. Mercer strung along that first boatload of girls too.

But Nettie goes on, "So, I decided to make one happen. The legislature will give in. They'll allot us some money and we'll build a school."

I decided to make one happen. Like Miss Gower and the lifeboat school.

"Why would Seattle build a university before they built a primary school? Or even a grammar school?"

Nettie chuckles. "That, m'dear, is a very long story. Let's just say the legislature dared us to, so we did. We do a lot of things well here. Civic planning isn't one of them."

"It's so pretty. Where are all the students?"

"Huh!" Nettie snorts. "There haven't been proper university students here in almost three years. I'd *like* to use one of the rooms to open a primary school, but the esteemed president does not see fit to entertain my request."

She makes a show of putting one hand to her ear and pointing it behind her, but there's no response from inside.

"I'll wear the old goat down and prevail in the end." Nettie winks. "If you're interested, I'm charging three dollars for the session."

It might as well be three hundred dollars. As far as I know, we still owe Mr. Mercer for our boarding bill on the *Continental*.

She said *prevail*, though. Nettie is trying to tell me something. Like Miss Gower and her big words.

"I could be your invigilator!" I straighten and grin big. "That would surely pay the cost. Right?"

Nettie frowns. "What's an invigilator?"

"For the little ones. A helper. Um. Someone to help . . . teach . . ." I trail off because Nettie is shaking her head.

"Not to hurt your feelings, but I can't imagine needing someone else to manage a schoolhouse in a town this size. Heavens, I wouldn't be much of a teacher if I did!"

She says the last part cheerfully, like she doesn't mean anything by it.

"Oh," I say quietly. "Oh."

I wouldn't think an experienced teacher like Miss Gower would need a helper for just ten children.

"You're more than welcome to join the class," Nettie adds.

"No I'm not," I mutter, and I slump as I turn on my heel and blindly rush down Third Avenue.

22

I PUSH OFF IN MY CANOE.

I wouldn't think an experienced teacher like Miss Gower would need a helper for just ten children. Because she didn't. Flora saw it right away. Miss Gower never needed my help.

Half the time I wasn't even helping. I was doing recitations and longhand division right alongside the boys.

I swing the oar from port to starboard and back, keeping a nice, steady course toward the Eastside. Stroke on stroke, just as good as chopping wood for getting angry thoughts out of my head.

She just felt sorry for me. *Poor dear.*

Your daughter is an excellent invigilator.

Still, Miss Gower called things as they were. If *invigilate* comes from Latin and means *to watch*, maybe that can mean a lot of things. Perhaps it's exactly what I did back on the *Continental*. Perhaps it's what I should do now.

I watched Miss Gower trick Mrs. D. Or maybe *trick* isn't the right word. It's not like I didn't earn that money. It was more like Miss Gower showed me a way to solve the problem that let all of us win. Mrs. D got something she wanted. I got something I wanted. Miss Gower got something too—she got to infuriate someone who insisted on preserving ignorance.

Miss Gower might have felt sorry for me, but maybe she felt angry for me too.

Soon, I spot a plume of red hanging on a tree. When I get closer, I recognize not only the stump dock, but the pattern of the cedars to the right of it. I glide my canoe up to the dock and climb out, then tie up far in the woods like Dad says to.

I stand on the dock and press my throbbing hands against my throbbing back.

I didn't get lost. I didn't fall in.

My canoe has changed everything.

It's also changed nothing.

Or maybe my canoe is like Miss Gower. It will give me a way to change everything. Just not the way I expected, and not without putting in the work.

❦ ❦ ❦

I put on my britches and hang my gown on its peg, then I find my hatchet and join Dad in the clearing where he's grubbing a stump.

"You're back early," he says. "Everything go all right?"

"I got the flour and oatmeal, just like you asked."

"You didn't need to hurry back." Dad pulls out a few pieces of charred stump and tosses them aside. "You might have passed some time with your friends."

"I couldn't. They were all in school." I kneel and help pry stump chunks. "Dad?"

Dad smiles all silly, just like he does when he says *Mrs. Wright*.

"School costs three dollars, and I know that's a lot of money, but may I go? A new session's starting soon."

Dad sits back on his heels and scrubs a handkerchief over his shiny forehead. "May you? I think you ought to. I never had much schooling myself. Being ignorant makes you powerless. You've got to place a lot of trust in anyone with more learning than you."

Like if you can't cipher and you need to reckon a debt. Like if you have to hit a sailor and you don't know to aim for his windpipe.

Papa wanted me to earn a leaving certificate because *when you educate a woman, you educate a family*. Dad is like Miss Gower—he would have me *prevail*.

"*Can* you?" Dad sighs. "If I had the money, it'd be yours. I spent what was left of my Fraser River savings on your boarding bill at the Occidental, though, and I owe Albert Pinkham for at least six months' worth of dry goods."

I hate money. I hate that everything has to cost, and I hate that it costs everyone the same when there are jobs for boys but not girls and pennypinchers charge high rent for a schoolroom.

"It's a long way to pull a canoe every day," Dad goes on. "Money aside, the trip would be hard on you. Soon enough it'll be raining all the time. You'll be drenched and muddy before you even step foot in the classroom."

I recite the reflection I wrote last week in the privy while waiting for a break in the sheeting, endless rain so I could get back to the cabin without being half-drowned.

"If you always wait for fair weather, you'll never get anything done."

Mr. W laughs, abrupt and unplanned. "You're definitely learning to be on the Pacific coast."

"So, I can go to school?" I press.

"We should talk it over with Mrs. Wright," he says, and this time he doesn't get all giggly. "It's got to do with money we don't have, and it's got to do with you."

I want to tell him not to bother. That I know what

she's going to say. *School's got nothing left to teach you, Jane. These dishes won't wash themselves, Jane.*

Just like Lowell.

Only it's not. This time, a grown-up is taking my side.

Jer and I are turned out of the cabin while Dad and Mrs. D *talk it over.* It's nice to play with Jer again. We play hide-and-seek and jump off stumps. We eat the wild salmonberries that weigh down the bushes along the edge of the clearing and stain our hands bright red. When we're stuffed, we fill a dishcloth with them, so I can make a crumble once I'm allowed back in the house.

It's forever before the door opens and Dad steps outside. "Mrs. Wright and I agree you may go to school if you keep up with your chores and find a way to pay the teacher yourself."

Then he sighs, runs a hand through his small bit of hair, and heads toward the trail that leads down to the long bank.

At supper Mrs. D talks only when she has to, and it's things like *please pass the wapatos* and *Jer, use your fork.*

It's three days before she says a single thing to me: *Don't think this gets you out of the dishes, miss.* Her voice is all warpy, like she's been crying.

At Ida's wedding I make sure to stand next to Nettie

Baker and find out when her school is starting. Nell's lavender muslin gown fits me better than I thought it would and reminds me I'll need a new dress for school, since showing up in my torn green rag will doubtless be frowned on.

Dad is a wreck with Mrs. D being mad at him. He brings her wildflowers and spends a whole afternoon putting a flagstone in front of the privy instead of checking the traps, but she stays angry.

"She'll come around," Dad says wearily as we watch Jer beat the bushes for rabbits on the evening before the first day of school. "Don't worry. Just go and study hard."

Now I almost don't want to go. I'm not sure what I'll come back to.

Only, I do. The cabin will be here. The long bank will be here. Dad will be here. No one puts this much time and sweat into something and just turns his back on it.

Maybe Mrs. D sees that too.

So, the next day I'm up at barely-dawn and pulling toward the camp landing in my dress that doesn't fit and a thirdhand pair of boys' loggingman boots. I've got a bucket of salmonberries and three eggs tied up in my handkerchief. They're not worth three dollars, but I'll just keep bringing Nettie things till she says it's enough.

There's only so many ways I can improve myself on

the Eastside. Only I wouldn't be here to broaden my mind with school if no one taught me to make a canoe or if I hadn't figured out where the best berries are.

Halfway up Third Avenue, I hear Nettie ringing the bell from the steps of the main university building. Kids are filing in, and I hurry to join them. Evie and Jenny take my elbows and pretend to get us stuck in the door as we walk in like they don't notice my dress is wet from the knees down where I knelt in my canoe.

There's a blackboard at the front of the room, maps hanging on the walls, and desks set up in rows with a space between to separate boys from girls. There's a big stove in the middle with cedar stacked up tidy around it. Nettie is buttoned-up perfect like Miss Gower and smiling like Miss Bradley.

Evie, Inez, and I sit in the same row. Madge is in front of us and Jenny is behind.

It's not schoolhouses on every corner, and I might be damp and slightly bedraggled, but I did my own pulling. I did my own berrying.

I am no one's *poor dear.*

The first week goes so well, I'm a bit sad when it's Friday. Saturday is nice because Dad and I take Jer down to the long bank to smoke fish with Lawrence and give Mrs. D some time to herself. Dad carries Jer on his shoulders, and I swing the bucket of salt and sing "Haul on the Bowline" like the deckhands on the *Continental* taught me and try to forget why she's so angry.

Mrs. D doesn't believe Papa wanted me to get a leaving certificate. She says things like *he married me, didn't he?*

Or rather, she used to. Back when she was still speaking to any of us.

I boil four of our nicest eggs and collect a healthy pailful of salmonberries for Miss Baker for the week. I pack it all careful and tuck a handkerchief over it to keep out lake water and bugs.

On Monday I make sure I get to school well before the bell, and I march up to Miss Baker's desk and proudly hold out the pail. "Here you are, ma'am!"

Miss Baker takes it, but her smile falters when she shifts the handkerchief. "Oh. Berries."

"Is something wrong with them?" I ask. "They didn't get smashed, did they?"

"No . . ." Miss Baker replaces the cloth and sets the pail on the floor. "Jane, honey. I . . . ah . . . haven't finished the berries you brought last week."

"Oh." I frown at the heaping bucket. "Can't you make a pie or something?"

"I did. Two, in fact."

The classroom is starting to fill up. Madge and Inez come in with Evie close behind, and I give them a little half wave because I planned to hand my week's tuition to Miss Baker before they were here to see me do it.

Miss Baker gestures me closer and lowers her voice. "These must go home with you. It's not fair to the others. You needn't pay your tuition all at once, but if you plan to stay—and I hope you do—I'll need some earnest money before the end of the month. At least a dollar. In coins."

The pair of socks I'm working on is barely a quarter done. All the storekeepers have more eggs than they know what to do with. Dad just traded our pile of pelts to Mr. Pinkham to pay the reckoning and get Mrs. D her calico.

"Yes, ma'am," I whisper, but it comes out all blubbery because I may or may not be crying in front of the whole class.

"I'm sorry, Jane. I really am." Miss Baker hands me her handkerchief because mine is stiff with dried berry juice. "Unfortunately, my landlady insists on actual currency in exchange for board. Otherwise all our lives would be easier."

My mind must be more shrinkened than I thought if I figured a pailful of stupid berries would be enough to pay an honest-to-goodness teacher, when Miss Gower handed me a dollar a week just to pretend.

I should have written this reflection long ago. The moment I learned the Washington Territory in Mr. Mercer's pamphlet was too good to be true. The moment I realized there are people in the world who lie for profit.

If something's not there to be had by anyone, you don't wait around for a banker to save you. You don't keep looking for palm trees. You don't fool yourself that you'll get a leaving certificate and keep a promise to a dead man.

You sit yourself quietly down with a simple, bitter truth. Sooner or later, you'll have to open your hand and let the whole silly notion go.

23

THE DAY STARTS OUT ALL RIGHT, FOR A DAY where Mrs. D still looks through Dad when he tries to dump buckets for her or pretends he doesn't want coffee so she can drink his share. For a day that's numbered, because the end of the month is approaching and I still don't have a coin to my name.

Telling Miss Baker will be hard. Telling Dad will be unbearable.

The sky is the color of dirty metal when I push away from the stump dock, and the wind off the lake cuts in a way it shouldn't in September. The wind is off my port beam and I have to pull against it to the camp landing, and I'm wet clear through from the spray by the time I've beached the canoe.

Miss Baker has me switch seats with Gretchen Clyde so I can be near the stove.

By recess that awful misting rain is falling. A hard drizzle starts up after lunch, the kind that bounces off everything from the roof to the fence to the mud. When school's out, the whole sky is open and Third Avenue is awash. Usually, the view's pretty from the university's porch, but today the bay is one long sheet of gray. You can't even see Port Madison out in the distance for the fog.

Evie pulls up her hood and ties it tight. "You want to stay the night at my house, Jane?"

I do. I'm almost dry, and I'll be drenched again even before I get to the camp landing. But if I can't make it home in a little rain, Dad might decide that my canoe will need to be permanently stowed till next summer.

Besides, he's probably had a long day of being ignored while I've been sitting with my friends at either elbow, in front of, and behind me.

"Thanks anyway," I reply, "but I'd better not."

I push off from the camp landing and start pulling, but the wind has picked up and it's hard to stay on course. It's too foggy for me to even make out the Indians' fishing island, but I know where it ought to be. The rain drills down, and it's hard to lift my arms in my wet cloak and dress.

Soon, I have to rest every ten strokes.

Then, every five strokes.

I can't rest. I have to keep pulling so I can get home. Only, pulling doesn't seem to work. Between the wind and the waves I might as well be anchored, and no amount of pulling's going to change that.

I should have stayed with Evie. I could be drinking hot tea and eating buttered toast and sending Felicity on a secret mission to stop a jewel thief.

It's going to be dark soon, and I can barely lift my arms. There's water in the bottom of my canoe as deep as my thumb. I don't know where I am. This might be only a lake, but it's a *big* lake.

The canoe's going to fill up. It's going to sink. I don't have the strength to right myself. Not now. Not soaking and sore.

Through the fog and wind-flung rain I can make out a spindly shape. It's like a tall spider standing in shallow water.

A dock. A proper dock made of pilings.

A dock's like a front door here on the lake. That's what Dad told me before we made this canoe.

Sitting on the dock are two boys holding fishing poles. At least I think they're boys. They look about my age, and they're wearing sailors' oilskins that in no way fit them, but that I suddenly envy because they must be warm and dry.

"Hey!" I call. "I'm lost! Can you help? Please?" Then I add, "*Mahsie? Tsolo . . . um . . . house? Elehan?*"

It's terrible Chinook, but one boy hands his pole to the other and shouts, "Over here!"

I pull toward the dock. I could weep for how much easier it is with the wind at my back instead of my face. As I get closer, the boys put their poles down and kneel, ready to catch the canoe when I'm near enough.

Finally—*finally*—I bump up to the dock. The boys tie the canoe in a trice, and it flails and bobs against the pilings from the force of the storm. It's all I can do to gather my sopping cloak about me and heave myself onto the boards.

"Oh, hey!" The taller boy is a little older than me, and he's got bronzy skin like an Indian but it's not as dark as most of the Indians' I've seen. His hair is long and fluttery under his big hat, and he's grinning like it's Christmas morning. "You're a girl!"

Any port in a storm, the deckhands on the *Continental* used to say, but right now I could very much do without Opinions on what girls should and shouldn't do.

But the younger boy goes on, "You've *got* to come to our cabin. Will you? Please? Hannah—that's our sister— Hannah hasn't seen another girl or lady or anyone, really—except our granddad and us—since she came to take care of us, and she used to be in a school all for girls, and she's sad because she misses them. The other girls. Not the school, though. She hated that place."

"Can I . . . yes, I'm happy to meet your sister." I swipe rain from my eyes. "I don't want to impose, though."

"Also, you should stay for dinner," the older boy says, and just the *thought* of food sets me hurrying up the path behind him.

By the time we reach the boys' cabin, I learn their name is Norley and that William just turned thirteen and Victor is ten. Their mama was an Indian and their dad was a white man and he got them this homestead claim and then both their parents died of a bad fever and Hannah had to be brought back from school to look after them, but even though they're happy to see her, they really don't need looking after because they're doing well enough on their own proving up this homestead; just look at all that fence and those strips of land under plow and not a stump in sight *thank you very much.*

When Victor throws open the cabin door, chattering how he and William caught a *strange fish*, a girl about the same age as my *Continental* friends turns from the busy stove. She's bronzy brown like her brothers, and her hair is braided and piled just like Nell's.

I stand there helplessly dripping on her nice, clean floor. Too cold and stiff and bone-tired to even mind my manners.

"A strange fish, indeed!" Hannah crosses the room in three strides and pulls me toward the stove. "Come warm yourself right now. Boys, mop up that water."

In two minutes she has me changed into one of her old dresses and my wet clothes hanging up to dry. At the same time, she's putting supper on the table and giving her brothers enough of a Look that they start washing their hands. Only, they're washing up in the murky dishpan, so she groans and shoves them outdoors with a cake of brown soap.

We're partway through a delicious supper of fish and biscuits and a conversation about people who live on the lake when William squawks, "Hey! She got in again. Get her, Vic!"

"Oh no," Hannah cries, and I swivel in my chair to see a nanny goat chewing a big hole in the front of my wet dress while trampling the skirts filthy.

Victor's up and cramming a biscuit in his mouth as he runs, but the goat takes off with my clothes trailing behind her like a fallen banner. He tries to pounce on the goat, but she darts to the left at the last minute, and he goes skidding into a big grandfather clock.

William slams the door shut and the goat prances backward, going *maaaa* like she knows how much trouble she's in. Victor drops a rope around her neck and both boys crow in victory. They push-pull the goat back outside. She takes a long scrap of my dress with her.

"I simply cannot believe that just happened." Hannah squinches up her face. "I'm so sorry. That goat is more trouble than she's worth. We've got four of them, but do any of the others break into the house and eat things that aren't food? No, sir. Just that one."

"My dress was mostly patches and bad seams anyway, and you saw how ill it fit." I give Nell's saucy grin, because Hannah's cheeks are red and she's toying with her mug.

"Still. You're a guest in my home. Please keep what you're wearing. I feel awful."

I pick up my piece of bread with a layer of butter so thick my teeth leave marks where I bite. "I can't imagine any animal that lets you have milk and butter could ever be more trouble than it's worth."

"You want her?"

I laugh, because Hannah's likely being funny.

"Offer something," she says. "Chances are good I'll take it."

"I doubt I have anything you want." Especially considering the berry pie on her stove behind me.

"Teach my brothers to read."

"*That's* worth a goat to you?" I ask.

"Most definitely."

I squint at her, but she's not teasing. "You went to school. Couldn't you teach them?"

Hannah shrugs. "It was a mission school. I learned to sew and pray."

"There's a school in town," I say, and it comes out sad, like I'm already out of time. "At the university. It costs money, but the teacher's nice."

"I doubt they'd be allowed to go." Hannah glances uneasily at the door and talks quietly even though William and Victor are still outside with the goat.

She says *doubt*, but she sounds pretty sure. At that town meeting in Seattle, Reverend Bagley had nothing nice to say about Indians and white people getting married. There have to be more kids like the Norleys if he's complaining so much. Kids whose minds get broadened only in ways that people like Reverend Bagley decide is good for them.

"Even if they were allowed," Hannah goes on, "can you see either one of them lasting five minutes in a classroom where they'd have to sit still and pay attention and study and recite?"

Something goes *kerthump* against the cabin wall, then a mudball sings past the front window. Moments later

William bursts through the door laughing, both arms filthy to the elbow. Victor barrels in after him with wads of mud clinging to his hair and shoulders.

"Out! Wash it off *outside*! And *you*"—Hannah stabs a finger at William—"will do the dishes tonight for that bit of meanness."

"Awwwww, we were only playing!" William protests, but he grumbles his way to the dishpan and flicks out his jackknife to shave some soap into the water.

Hannah turns to me. "Teaching those two to read will be a piece of work, but if you'll do it, you can take that awful goat with you this very moment. I mean, when the rain lets up."

"Sure," I say, mostly because I don't like the idea of anyone having to look in a schoolhouse window and not being allowed to go inside, but also because if we have a goat, I can sell cheese and butter to Mr. Pinkham and pay Miss Baker with coins. "Only, I can't take the goat with me this very moment, because I have no idea where home is from here. I wish I did. I'll be missed."

As soon as I say it, I reckon how long it's been since school got out. Here I've been, eating supper without even a thought for how frantic they must be.

"Our granddad can take you home," Hannah replies. "Victor, go see if Granddad is back yet."

Victor gives a cheerful salute, puts on his oilskins, and disappears out the door.

Hannah and I agree that I'll come over every Saturday to teach William and Victor. I clear the supper dishes while she fixes a heaping plate for her grandfather and sets it on the back of the stove to keep warm.

"I can teach them ciphering, too. So they can know if anyone's trying to cheat them. Also . . ." I pause, because I'm not sure how to say it without sounding rude. "If you want to learn too, that's fine with me."

"I'll think about it," Hannah says, but she also smiles real shy like she's glad I'm coming at all.

Victor bangs through the door, leaving it open behind him. The sky is more than passing dark now, and I'm glad I'll have an escort home, because there's no way I'd find my way in the dark *and* the rain.

An older man in oilskins comes in behind Victor, and I blurt, "Lawrence!"

His brows go up when he sees it's me, and he says something to Hannah in Lushootseed. She nods and replies. Then Lawrence smiles and gestures at the door.

I hug Hannah and thank her for everything—supper, her old dress, the goat.

I wonder if she likes to knit.

Down at the dock Lawrence ties a long rope between

our canoes. Victor and William have tethered the goat into their granddad's weather-beaten bow. The poor thing is already dripping from her ears and tail and belly-hair.

"*Mamook isick.*" Lawrence makes a paddling motion with his oar.

I nod. He's telling me that I have to pull too, that he'll be guiding me and not dragging me. "*Mahsie*, Lawrence. Really."

We pull. The rain sheets down.

It feels like forever before Lawrence starts moving toward shore. The stump dock is completely underwater, so he finds a place where I can leap from root to root and scrabble up to damp land. Then he tosses my mooring rope, and while I'm securing my canoe, he hoists the goat up on shore. Even though she's pitiful and shivering, the rope around her neck trailing like she just escaped the hangman, I could swear she's glaring at me.

"*Kloshe chako?*" Lawrence calls.

"Yes, I'm all right. *Kloshe chako. Mahsie hyiu!*"

He waves his oar, then points his canoe away from land. I wrap the goat's rope double around my hand and tug her up the lake path toward home.

THE CABIN WINDOWS GLOW ALL THE WAY FROM the head of the lake trail. It's hard to move. The shock of leaving the Norleys' warm kitchen and getting soaked and windblasted once more left me boneless.

I drag through the clearing, towing the goat, and push the cabin door open.

Mrs. D and Dad are sitting together on the hearth bench. He's not whittling. She's not knitting. They're holding hands and staring at the fire.

Jer is belly-down on his bed, playing with Hoss and Other Hoss, but he must feel the draft, because he looks up and squeals, "Daney!"

Dad is across the room in an instant. He pulls me inside the cabin, goat and all, and throws his arms around me. He doesn't even seem to care that I'm soaking wet and dripping all over the floor. I hug him back.

"Daney! Daney!" Jer squeezes my leg, then pulls away. "Ugh. You all wet."

Mrs. D scrubs at her eyes as she waits for a turn to hug me, and she gives me a proper hug too, like she'd give Jer.

"Charles went over to Seattle to look for you when you didn't come home on time," she says. "I thought for sure you'd stayed to play with one of your friends without a thought or care for anyone who might be worried about you."

She's speaking to me. She's calling Dad *Charles* instead of *Mr. Wright*.

She was worried about me.

Dad runs a hand through his damp hair. Quietly, he says, "Your canoe wasn't at the landing."

I know what he's not saying in front of Jer, and I'm glad for it. *I thought you capsized. I thought you drowned.*

"I won't ever stay after school without telling you," I promise, and I mean it. "I'm sorry for worrying you. I—"

"Why in heaven's name do you have a *goat?*" Mrs. D's voice is back to its old, unsentimental grating.

"Oh." I look down at the rope in my hand. "Oh! She's our goat now. Milk and butter and cheese!"

I tell them how the wind pushed me and it was foggy

and I lost my way and met the Norleys—did they know Lawrence is a granddad?—and agreed to teach the boys in return for a—

"Hey!" Jer yanks his nightshirt out of the goat's mouth. "Bad goat!"

"—goat," I finish. "We should pen her up in one of the sheds right away, because Jer's right. She doesn't know how to behave."

"Bad goat," Jer mutters, glaring at her.

Dad puts on his overcoat and takes Bad Goat outside while I peel off my wet clothes behind the curtain.

When I come out in my nightdress, Mrs. D is waiting, arms folded. "You scared the daylights out of Mr. Wright. You scared the daylights out of *me*. And for what?"

She knows very well what. She just can't see why.

I'm trying to find the strength to *yes no I don't know ma'am* her, when she goes on quietly, "Do you really hate me so much? Would it be so terrible if you were more like me?"

She's not giving me a Look. Her face is open and sad. Betrayed, even.

There's no right answer.

"Because I can't think of another reason you'd insist on doing the things you do. There's nothing special about book learning. There's nothing ladylike about traps and the woodpile." Then she adds in a soft voice, "There's nothing wrong with keeping house."

"I can't be you." I'm tired enough to be honest. "I don't know how. I want to be me."

Mrs. D sighs. "I don't know what to make of you sometimes."

No. I don't think she would. Maybe she doesn't want to. She likely never had a Miss Gower or a dad. No one's ever asked what she thought. If no one helps you prevail, maybe it helps to convince yourself you're better off than anyone who does.

"I don't know what to make of you a lot of the time." I say it nice but maybe that's not enough, so I add, "Ma'am."

Mrs. D coughs a laugh just like Nell might, and that's when I remember she's not much older than Nell. Or me.

"Well, we're here now." Mrs. D waves a hand like she's pointing at the whole Eastside. "This place will make of us what it will."

It won't, though. It can't. Washington Territory is only a place. A lovely place, sure, but it can't change everything. That has to come from you.

Now that I've agreed to teach William and Victor, all I can think about is how I have no books. Not that you need them to teach someone to read, but if the Norley boys can't have a real teacher, at the very least they should learn with proper books.

Jenny has a first reader, but her little brother needs it. Evie can't remember what became of hers. I ask Nell, not because I think it's likely she'd have books to lend, but because she's got a dozen suitors, and every last one would produce *ten* readers if she dropped the smallest of hints.

"You should talk to Ida. She's got a whole rucksack full of schoolbooks, and it's unlikely she's reading them for pleasure." Nell picks at a knot in the fishing net she's mending. "Plus, I might have mentioned how upset you were that she didn't invite you to her school. So she's likely looking for a way to make it up to you."

I groan and shove Nell playfully, but one day after school, I go to Pinkham's General Store. Ida is sweeping the porch, bundled in the lovely woolen cape that marks her a back Easterner from fifty yards away.

"Jane!" Ida leans the broom against the building and beckons me up the steps. "Nell told me everything. I'm sorry. I really am. But—"

"I know, *but.*" I pat Ida's arm to let her know I'm not mad, and this time I really do mean it. Between my canoe and Dad, there will be fewer buts in the future.

"You really ought to start paddling in more often." Ida says it like it's no more odd than walking up the block and around the corner. "Nell and Sarah and I need a better fourth than Kitty McEvoy. Besides, we've missed you."

"I'll try," I promise, although I'll be *pulling* and not *paddling*. Schoolteachers know a lot of things, but even they can broaden their minds on occasion. "Say, is there any chance you'd lend me your books? Your readers and spellers, I mean, from when you were teaching."

Ida scrunches her nose. "I imagine it would get tiresome all alone in the wilderness without anything to look at. So yes, I don't see why not. I shouldn't need them back till . . . well . . . till there's a child who might like to look at them."

"Thanks," I tell her, and before I can add how I won't just be reading them myself, she's gone all pink and bashful and ducked into the store.

Before long she's back with a satchel that weighs down her arm something fierce. Under a pile of novels I'll never read, there's *all six* McGuffey Readers, two spellers, a Mitchell's *Geography*, and a lovely old primer that will be perfect for William and Victor.

On Saturday I'm up early and pulling to the Norley dock with Ida's primer and McGuffey's First Reader. I'm not anything like a proper teacher, but Hannah's right. William and Victor wouldn't do well with someone like Miss Bradley or Miss Gower. They need a teacher who will let them wiggle and twitch as they chant A, B, C. Someone who can figure out a way to teach them, so each of us gets something we want.

The boys are waiting for me on the dock. Right away they ask do I want to see an apple as big as my head.

"There's no such thing," I reply, but they walk me through their small orchard and sure enough, there are several ridiculously large apples under a gnarly old tree. Victor makes a gift of one, and I have to take it in both hands.

"This will make my brother giggle like a fool," I say, and both boys beam and start elbowing each other. "We really should start the lessons, though."

Victor sighs noisily. William's face falls, but he's polite enough—or worried enough about Hannah's wooden spoon upside his ear—that he just nods.

"I thought maybe we could have lessons outside," I go on. "Right here, in your orchard."

"Really?" William perks up. "Hannah cleared off the table, but being outside would be much better."

"Yeah!" Victor plops down without me having to ask. So we do.

I wouldn't exactly call William and Victor *willing* pupils. Their learning to read is clearly Hannah's idea, but by noon, they can manage the alphabet reliably. Pictures worked with Milly and Maude, but William and Victor do better when I have them run between trees, hitting the trunks each time they say a letter.

We move inside after dinner. I pour a handful of silty sand on two cedar planks, and the boys practice drawing letters in it. Hannah comes over to watch, toying with a washrag. She hovers till I slide a board with sand in front of her, and she joins her brothers, carefully making letters, then smoothing out the sand to write the next one.

"Supper will be ready soon." Hannah nods toward the wapatos and venison cooking in a shallow dish on the stove. "You're welcome to stay."

"Tempting, but I'd best be off before it gets too dark. Lawrence likely has better things to do than see me home again." I turn to William and Victor. "You both did very well today. I'm pleased with how hard you're both working."

Victor frowns at the sandy boards. "You really mean that? You're not just saying that because we're friends?"

"Of course I mean it," I say, because William is nodding skeptically and mostly I'm surprised that they consider me a friend when I haven't known them very long and I'm their teacher, sort of.

Then again, there's nothing wrong with learning from your friends. So I add, "It's best to call things as they are.

So yes, you both did well and no, I'm not saying that just because we're friends."

The boys grin, and it occurs to me they might not have a lot of company besides each other. They might be just as happy to have a new friend as Hannah is.

I remind William and Victor to work on making letters in the sand all week. I leave the primer so they have something to copy. They walk me down to the dock, chattering over each other like jackdaws. I tuck my head-size apple in the bow to keep it safe.

Jer hugs the apple like it's a rabbit. He cries when Mrs. D wants to make it into applesauce. He tucks it into his bed along with Hoss and Other Hoss.

"How it get big?" Jer asks. "We have another?"

"I don't know," I tell him, "but I know two boys who might."

I'm pretty sure they'll tell me if I ask. It's the sort of thing a friend would do.

25

IT'S STILL DARK WHEN MRS. D NUDGES ME AWAKE. I wash up, then go take care of Bad Goat. Two new batches of goat cheese are ready to go to Mr. Pinkham's store. Hannah showed me how to make molds out of old tin cans, and I drew some crooked pictures of them in my reflections on Homesteading.

All the way up Third Avenue I jingle the coins in my skirt pocket that I got from Bad Goat's cheese. I'll be able to give them to Miss Baker for tuition.

I'll be able to stay on that hard school bench with my friends.

At noon we sit on the porch and unpack our dinners. Below, Seattle is busy. Bustling, even. Some boys are digging for clams, the millhands are turning out pilings, and a handful of Chinese men are setting puncheon logs into the mud in front of Mr. Horton's store to make a sidewalk.

"Digging clams looks like more fun than eating them," I say. "Hey, will one of you teach me how?"

Evie wrinkles her nose. "I have no idea how to dig clams, and I don't care at all to learn."

Jenny wiggles her fingers at me. "I can do without the blisters. I'd rather read."

"You already know how to read," I point out.

"Next thing we know, Jane will want to learn to set puncheons," Evie teases. "It'll be her and Mr. Ling and Mr. Han and their boys."

The other girls laugh and shoulder-bump me playfully, but saplings cut in half and buried so the cut sides line up flat and perfect could firm up the long bank or even the lake trail.

I would. I *would* like to learn to set puncheons.

I love Evie dearly. Jenny, too. But preserving your ignorance only leaves you at the mercy of someone else, and you'll be very lucky if they merely call you *poor dear* and leave you alone.

I might never get a leaving certificate. I don't even know if schools like Miss Baker's can give them. The whole Pacific coast is my schoolhouse, though, and I'll never be done learning.

That afternoon Miss Baker calls on me to recite. I stand and read my assigned passage without missing a single word.

Not even the big ones.

When it's Madge's turn, I sneak my pamphlet out of my dress pocket and open it in my lap. I write a new reflection.

There is more than one way for a girl to broaden her mind.

It's Sunday. I've been turned out of the cabin so Mrs. D can take a bath in the tin washtub. Dad took Jer down to the long bank, just the two of them.

I wander out toward the salmonberry patch with my carpetbag over my shoulder. I take out my reflections and flip through the pages. My chapters on Homesteading and Food and Canoeing are filled in pretty well, and School is coming along nicely. My penmanship isn't the best and my spelling would never pass even the kindest teacher, but everything I've written goes from margin to margin. No corrections or improvements here.

Unlike Mr. Mercer's stupid pamphlet. I pull that one out and put it next to my little book. His is shabby and dingy, but it still looks like a proper pamphlet. The cover is made of stiff yellow paper and the printing is all just so.

My little book is also grubby, but that's because my

hands are not always clean when I write reflections. The pages don't line up properly because they're folded rag-paper, and my title on the cover—*REFLECTIONS ON WHAT'S NOT GOING*—starts out big and then gets smaller as I got near the edge and ran out of room.

I pick up Mr. Mercer's pamphlet. I don't know why I even still have it. I should have flung it into the lake weeks ago.

I turn to the Introduction and run a finger over words I already know by heart: *It is my hope that in these pages my readers will discover the wealth of potential and possibility inherent in the material resources of the northwest corner of this great land.*

There's no correction. No improvement. I read that first line again.

Potential.

Possibility.

I open my little book to the chapter on Seattle. It's a full five pages long, and I've drawn a picture of the streets and buildings from the top of the mill road and labeled each one. I've listed all the stores and which are best to buy ribbons or candy, and which give the best prices for milk and cheese. I've written out words in Chinook by how they sound, and what they mean in English.

There's a single line in Mr. Mercer's pamphlet about

Seattle. One solitary mention tucked away in the chapter on Trade discussing the quality of its harbor. I flip through the pages twice, but I've read them enough times to know what's here.

Then I turn each one slowly. Everything is just as I remember it. Grazing Land. Whale Fishing. Charts full of numbers, like how many boards you can get from a cedar of a certain width.

Nothing about bankers or bachelors. Not a single word about schoolhouses.

I close the cover gently. It's not lies. Not really. This is the Washington Territory Mr. Mercer sees. He's called things as they are, just like Miss Gower said to. I'm the one who read those words so many times that I came to expect Washington Territory to be as I wanted it to be, not as it really is.

My pamphlet, though. My pamphlet isn't lies, either, even though the things I've written are different from Mr. Mercer's. My Washington Territory is full of stumps to grub and canoes to pull and traps to check and school to go to and new friends to knit with and teach their letters and old friends to play dolls and whist with.

I draw thick lines through my pamphlet's old title. Under it I write an improvement: *REFLECTIONS ON GOING FORTH.*

❦ ❦ ❦

Miss Baker dismisses school after dinner. She feels feverish and can't get warm. The smaller kids run whooping down the hill toward town while Jenny puts the fire out, Inez washes the blackboard, and I bring in wood for tomorrow.

Then we realize we have a whole afternoon to ourselves, because our parents think we're in school.

"Let's go play dolls!" Evie says happily. "The fearless Prince Pierre was in trouble, remember? Trapped in that cave by bears? Felicity and Sarabelle and the others were the only ones who could save him."

Mrs. D has her hearth. She might not be patting me on the head and telling me to go play, but she did say I could stay after school when I liked as long as my chores were done by bedtime. She might have said it with Dad standing at her elbow and giving her a Look, but she said it nonetheless.

Jer has his mama, but he doesn't need her quite like he used to. Or me, if I'm honest. He's not a baby anymore. He's a little boy now and his own man, and the only times he really needs one of us are when he's hurt or scared or hungry. He can make birdcalls and play in the mud and build little houses out of wood scraps. He knows which berries to eat and which to leave alone, and when to hurry into the house.

He's learning to be on the Pacific coast.

I have ordinary chores. I have wood to chop and stack. I have traps to check. I have furs to stake out and cure and treat. I have dishes to wash and drawers to scrub. On the Pacific coast a girl can fish for kokanee in the morning, smoke it in the afternoon, and serve it for supper that evening. She can pick berries and make a crumble and pull to school in her very own canoe.

So, I go to Evie's house. Felicity distracts the bears with a bucket of fresh dewberries while Sarabelle rushes into the cave, splints Prince Pierre's broken leg with cedar poles, then hurries him into a waiting canoe. Meanwhile, Hyacinth has gone back to their homestead cabin and convinced all the salmon in the sound to help them trick the bears into swimming to an island where they'll be trapped forever.

Before I know it, the sun's getting low on the horizon. I thank Mrs. Mason on my way out.

As I head toward the mill road, I pass Nell on the Occidental's common. She's with a young man and they're picnicking even though it's cold and beginning to spit rain. Perhaps he's not as boring as the last one. I wave and she waves back, then she makes a little motion of dealing cards with that spy-mission grin. I nod and call, "Sunday!"

My canoe is just as I left it, carefully rolled on its side to keep the rain out and tethered to a sapling. I slide it into the water and push off for home.

Near the Norley dock, Victor and William are fooling about in their canoe. As I pull past, Victor shifts abruptly and they both tumble into the lake. They come up sputtering and arguing, though, so I keep going. I'll see them this Saturday for lessons, and for dinner and checkers and knitting, too. Hannah can knit circles around me, and I'm doing my best to learn from her, since her socks sell for twice what mine do at Mr. Pinkham's.

The lake is especially busy this afternoon, and there are three canoes and a flat-bottomed boat and a weary-looking coal mover from Coal Creek pulling slow but steady for the camp landing. I turn and mark the smoke rising from chimneys on the Seattle side—the Norleys', the Grahams', the Cartwrights'. Others I don't know yet, but will soon enough. The lake's not that big a place after all.

Then I face forward. Toward the bushy green strip of cedar that's the Eastside. Even though I don't need the scrap of red cloth to mark our dock anymore, I leave it there because it's pretty. Also, in case anyone's ever out on the lake and wants to come to our front door.

Mrs. D will be cooking the kokanee Dad and I caught. She'll have them on cedar planks on a fire in the yard.

The whole clearing will smell like smoke, but in the very best way. Or she'll be in the garden, pulling a handful of turnips or onions to make hash. Or she'll be peeling wapatos out on the step.

Maybe she'll be smiling.

Dad will be on the edge of the clearing, grubbing a stump or chopping a tree. Or he'll be coming up the long bank path with a string of muskrat or a sackful of wapatos on his back. Or he'll be making cedar shakes to stack in his canoe and sell along with our skins and cheese in Seattle.

I know for a fact he'll be smiling.

Jer will be looking for rabbits or whacking things with his favorite stick or feeding wapato peelings to Bad Goat. When I come crunching up the lake path, he'll run over to me shouting, "Daney! Daney!"

In a few years Jer will be in the canoe beside me as I pull toward school. A few years after that, maybe I'll help him make his own canoe. Along with Lawrence, of course, and our dad.

I glide my paddle through the water, stroke by stroke. There's no sandy beach in sight. No palm trees or bankers, and the only schoolhouse is borrowed.

Instead, there's the timber and fur that provide my education. There's Evie and Jenny. There's Nell. There are the Norleys. There's my complicated, ramshackle family doing its best to be sturdy like the long bank and not like the rest of the shoreline where you must constantly watch how you step.

All of them together means I can finally call Washington Territory what it is.

Home.

Thanks so much to

Katherine Longshore, Jeannie Mobley, and Megan Morrison for their valuable feedback on drafts of this book at all stages of its creation.

The staff and librarians at the University of Washington, the Washington State Library, and the Seattle Public Library for connecting me with so many useful resources. A special thanks to Jade D'Addario in the Special Collections department at the Seattle Public Library for her help in providing me with access to early images of that city.

Cecile Hansen, chair of the Duwamish tribe, for her time and willingness to provide insights into the cultural representation of the indigenous peoples appearing in *The Many Reflections of Miss Jane Deming*.

My agent, Ammi-Joan Paquette, for her supportive

guidance, her never-failing enthusiasm, and her general awesomeness.

My editor, Reka Simonsen, for her particular brand of wisdom, patience, and intuition that made this book turn out a thousand times better than it would have on its own.

The team at Atheneum for all their hard work making this book lovely to look at and ready for the world.

The readers, authors, librarians, educators, and booksellers who make up the kidlit community. I'm so glad you've invited me in.